Derek Smith has lived most of his life in the East End of London. He has for many years been involved in community projects in the area, including being writer-in-residence for Soapbox Theatre and one of the founders of Page One bookshop in Stratford. He has had plays performed on radio, television and the stage, and has published seven books for children, including three novels by Faber.

Other children's books by Derek Smith:

Hard Cash
Half a Bike
Frances Fairweather Demon Striker!
The Good Wolf
Fast Food

For younger children:

The Magical World of Lucy-Anne
Lucy-Anne's Changing Ways
Jack's Bus

Baker's Boy

Derek Smith

Earlham Books

Published 2010
Earlham Books, London
Cover & design by Lia Rees

ISBN: 978-0-9536283-6-0

Chapter 1

My mother was a baker and a fine one too. So was my father, but he had to fight for the King – and died when I was little. I can't remember much of him, his big arms, his apron and the flour in his curly hair. So it's Mum and me had to run our shop. Well hardly a shop, our kitchen – the door always open so people could come in, but also to get rid of the heat from cooking. We did deliveries – well I did, not Mum – she cooked. And specials for the market, pies and cakes and rolls. I was learning to be a baker, would have been a baker but my life took a very different route. And this is how it came about.

One morning I had to go off to the windmill to get flour. I used to go about once a week. I set off with the wagon, and our horse, Oak. Called Oak because he was a deep brown and had legs like tree trunks. He was older than me, was Oak, and only had one pace, dead slow. Well that suited me. I enjoyed going up to the mill, made me feel grown up, on the cart on my own. Out in the open air, not so nice in winter when I'd wrap up in everything I had, but on a summer's day like this it was beautiful, rolling through the hedgerows. Oak knew the way. I had a whip, never used it, and I doubt it would've worked anyway.

Jed was the miller. He was a friend of my father, friend of the family really. He always asked about Mum, whether I was courting yet – all that teasing stuff. Him and his missus would always make me a drink, and give me whatever they were having themselves. To tell you the truth I was quite keen on their daughter, Rose. I think she liked me too, but we were both as shy as fallow deer. Long time ago, she's got four kids now. We both had other fancies since.

We loaded up the flour, six big sacks. Oak had had his feed and been watered, so I said my goodbyes and headed back. Slow and easy. It was May time; hawthorn flowers were in the hedgerow and stitchwort and red campion sticking their heads above the grass. Trees were fresh light green. All I had to do was sit on the board with the sun in my face, and Oak plodding as if heading to the end of the Earth, rather than the couple of miles to the village.

We were about halfway when the wind hit. It came from nowhere and almost blew me off the seat. I hung on with both hands. It was as hot as if Mother had just flung open the oven door. And troubled Oak, who whinnied and shook in the shafts. The noise of it was strange, like the wind through a gorge. It grew dark and I thought, there's going to be a terrible storm with thunder and lightning. It was then I looked up.

And saw the creature blocking out the sun. It was about the length of five wagons, with spikes down its back, growing smaller and disappearing along its lashing tail. Its belly was white and the rest of it purple. The wind came from its great wings, and the heat from the fire and smoke that poured from its mouth and nostrils. As for the rest of the head, pretty soon I was granted a closer view, as a great claw came down, grasped me, and drew me up to its yellow eyes while I trembled from head to foot. There it inspected me, like a cat with a mouse, deciding where to begin – the head or the feet. The decision made – it was to be the head – I was brought to the mouth. The sight of the vast jaw filled me with horror, the upper teeth hanging like pointed stalactites from a red cavern lit at the back by a glowing fire. Was this to be the end of my short life? I had hardly done anything. But it was not the time for regrets, I had no wish to be chewed and roasted. In my pocket were two rolls Mother had given me. I threw them. The first bounced off a tooth and hit me on the head, the least of my troubles. The second went into the mouth, hit the tonsils at the back and fell into the windpipe. All at once the dragon was thrown into a paroxysm of writhing. And I was dropped.

It was a long fall from the creature's jaw, but luckily for me I landed on the flour sacks. I rolled off, under the wagon and watched as the creature choked. Its head thrust backwards and forwards, wings flapping wildly, tail thrashing like a whip while it gurgled and spat. And then like a cannonball the burnt bread roll shot out its mouth and hurtled into the sky.

The dragon shook itself as it recovered. Its writhing had taken it well past me. And it seemed I was forgotten, for it headed in the direction of the village. I came out from under the wagon and ran after. To do what, I had not thought. It would be too late to warn anyone, but my mother was in the village, even now at her stove. And she was the only relative I had.

I was a mile or so away and the creature arrived long before I did. I could hear screaming as I approached, see the fire above the burning houses, and the creature darting into the streets and coming up with a mouthful of bodies kicking and struggling, before they were sucked in. Rapidly the smoke covered everything, except the roaring of the creature and the cries of the villagers.

By the time I got there, much of the village was ablaze. Some streets I could not go down because of the fire. Others, the smoke forced me back. But by heading this way and that, going anyway I could, I made my way to our cottage.

The house was burning. I could not even get close. The thatch was ablaze, inside was a furnace. If Mother was there then she was burnt to a cinder. I ran round the outside, trying to peer in the windows with the fire leaping up the walls, inside and out.

It was then I heard a cry from our garden. I rushed there. It was Mother's voice...

'Help me! Help me!'

...coming from our well. I was there in a few strides and looked down. There she was, way down, sitting on the bucket at the end of the rope, her feet in the water.

'Pull me up, son,' she called, her voice ringing round the wall.

I did so.

She came out wet, her hair a little singed – but not hurt at all. We hugged and thanked heaven. Our relief and explanations were interrupted by the ringing of the church bells. We were being summoned.

We ran through the burning streets to the village square.

There we found a sooty and dishevelled band, others coming to join them. Some we could not at first recognise although they were our customers and neighbours, they were so dirty and so miserable. It was the Mayor who had called us. His robes were burnt, his hair singed and face grimy. Usually he tried to keep some ceremony in his office but today he had none at all. He was as wrecked as we all were. Later I found out that his wife and son were victims of the dragon. There were many missing. Perhaps half the village were in attendance – the rest had been eaten or died in the fires.

The Mayor set us to work. It was the best thing for us. We must save what we could of the village. He formed us into parties, each to work together to put out fires in various areas. Mother and I were put with ten others. We gathered buckets and basins, whatever we could, formed a chain to the nearest well – and set to putting out the blaze. We worked all night. Mother stopped after a few hours and baked some bread for everyone in the village. Oak had come back with the wagon of flour – and there was no shortage of fire to cook on. It was hot, delicious bread and appreciated by everyone.

By morning we had done all we could. We sat together in the village square, exhausted. No one wanted to go back home, that's if they had homes to go to; we needed each other's company. Some slept, some sat numb waiting for those who would never come again.

The Mayor would not let us rest, or himself. He knew if he stopped he would collapse. Half the village had been saved. Some were fortunate, but Mother and I, like many others, had lost all we owned.

The Mayor rose unsteadily to his feet.

'Thank you all for your hard work.'

No one said anything. What else could we have done?

'But our task isn't over,' he went on.

Everyone knew that. There were houses to be built. Funerals to be arranged. Lives to be rearranged.

'The creature knows where we are,' said the Mayor. 'He knows we are weak.' Looking around at the sooty faces, their bodies slumped – everyone could see how weak we were.

'I need volunteers,' he said.

Heads shook, eyes looked at feet and fingernails.

'To kill the dragon before he kills us all.'

The silence was deafening. Eyes closed in pasty, tired faces. The Mayor sunk to his knees and suddenly wept.

It was then I rose.

'I volunteer,' I said.

No one looked at me. My legs were shaking. How had these words come out? Where had they come from?

The Mayor withdrew his hands from his face.

'Are you sure, Will?'

He was giving me the chance to withdraw.

'I am sure,' I said. As sure as a baby bird about to launch itself from a cliff.

'And so am I.'

Everyone looked at the resolute speaker.

It was Mother.

'We shall go together,' she said.

Half of me hated her for that. I wanted to be the hero of the village. And how can a hero set off with his mother? And yet I was glad too, for I desperately wanted company. And if there were no one else – then my mother it would be.

We set off quickly.

Mother took a rolling pin. It had terrified me as an infant, perhaps it would terrify a dragon. I brought a kitchen knife, Mother always demanded they be kept sharp. A blunt knife is only good for cutting pastry, she said.

The dragon's trail was not hard to follow. But what a dismal march! There were burning houses, burning trees. Fields aflame and charred. There were bones and bits of clothing lying on the wayside. And all along the way were weeping and wailing people by burnt out cottages. We had no need to ask why.

Here and there were huge footprints and the draggings of the tail. Mother and I barely spoke. It was if we had entered the gates of Hell and were on our way to meet the Devil himself who would further punish us. And yet we must make the journey.

We came to the foot of a mountain which was grey with ash. A little way off was an old man, rakish thin, with not a single hair on his head but with a long white beard. He was bent over, scooping up ash and letting it run through his bony fingers.

When he saw us, he called, 'Help me. I've lost my stick.'

'You silly old man,' retorted Mother. 'Just back in that village are people who have lost their houses and their families. And you are upset about a stick.'

'Help me,' he ordered.

'No,' said Mother.

The old man turned to me. 'Will you help me, young man?'

I looked to Mother. She shook her head vehemently.

I said, 'It is easier to find a stick, than find a dead family. I'll help you.'

And I began searching.

'And will you help, missus?'

'No,' said Mother. And she turned away.

I scuffed the ash with my feet. It was fine and light. Nothing grew.

'There used to be a forest here,' said the old man. 'And up the mountain too. But a hundred years ago, the dragon burnt it down.'

'Where does he live?' I said.

The old man pointed. 'Up there. See that cave? That's his den. He's there now, fat and sleepy.'

I looked for an hour for that stick. It was easier than going up the mountain. I think I would have stopped my searches but Mother was standing with her back to us, arms folded. And if I were to be told off for being foolish – then I'd rather I found the stick.

And I did.

'Is this it?' I picked up a twisted stick.

And the old man jumped for joy.

He took the stick, yelled some strange words and in a swoosh grew two feet taller. His dishevelled clothing became robes of yellow and blue. Then with a further wave of the twisted stick there appeared a small fire with three stools round it. He pointed one out, I sat down. Then another for Mother. She looked rather ashamed, and at first would not.

'Sit,' he insisted.

And she did so. Once all three of us were seated plates of food appeared in our hands. And we ate. Delicious food, so welcoming. All we'd eaten on the trail was bread and water, but here was meat and vegetables in a sweet gravy. Once the plate was empty, I turned to thank our host.

'Eat your food,' he said.

I looked back at my plate; it was full again. I ate my fill once more. The plates flew off and there appeared in our hands cups of golden cider which we gratefully drank. I began to thank him, but he stopped me with a raised hand.

'It is I must thank you,' he said, 'For two days I have been looking for my stick. These old eyes are not what they were.' From the pocket of his deep robes, he drew out a pair of black shoes. 'Give me yours,' he said.

I took mine off – and he threw them in the fire. And handed me the new pair. They were soft and furry but not made of fur, nor of any skin I knew. I slipped them on. They were snug to my feet, as if made for me and no one else.

'Wear no other pair,' he said.

'But his feet are still growing,' said Mother.

'They will grow with his feet,' he said. 'Scrunch your toes three times,' he said to me.

I did.

And instantly rose into the air. I was at first alarmed but it felt so natural, that without thinking I flew up higher, round the fire and back to my stool.

'They are my gift to you, baker's boy. Use them wisely.'

And with a wave of his stick the fire went, the magician too – and lastly the stools, leaving us seated on the ashy ground by ourselves.

We rose and began our trek up the mountain.

The ash was up to our ankles in places, amidst stumps of charred trees. It swirled in the air, creating a fog smelling of ancient burning. But there could be no more fires on this mountain. All that could be burnt was burnt.

We climbed for perhaps an hour, getting closer to the cave. Puffs of rhythmic smoke came from the entrance, suggesting the dragon was asleep. And closer still we heard the rumble of his snores.

Breathless after our climb, we stood a little back from the cavern, wondering how to begin.

'I'll go in and stir him,' I said.

'And when he comes out,' Mother said, 'I'll whack him with my rolling pin.'

The plan seemed unlikely, but so was our mission – and we had no better one. So I made my way to the entrance. The cavern was vast like the hall of a cathedral. And there in its midst lay the dragon, flat out on its back, wings folded, mouth opening and shutting as it snored and blew out smoke. The yellow eye, on the side of the face I could see, was open – but I realised it could see nothing. The creature had no eyelids.

I came in as close as I dared. There were bones lying here and there. I threw one and retreated like an infant playing grandma's footsteps. But it had no effect on the monster, simply bouncing off its body. I came in closer still and aimed for the wide-open eye. It was as big as a shield and difficult to miss.

And I didn't.

The animal woke with a bellow of rage. And I raced to the entrance. Once there, I scrunched my toes three times and was in the air. Below me was Mother waving her rolling pin. Immediately after me came the creature, straight up into the air. I was sure it recognised me, the tiny being it had held to its eyes and just missed eating.

It meant not to miss again.

The dragon and I flew about the mountain. I was much smaller and able to twist and turn, but was amazed by the dragon's strength and agility. I flew round the peak. And round. My plan was to get the animal giddy. The only trouble was I was growing giddy myself. I turned to look and could see its eyes rolling. I hoped it was worse off than I was.

I stopped in mid air; the creature was tottering, rocking from side to side. And there was Mother, clambering up the rock towards it, her rolling pin in one hand. The dragon could see her but was still recovering from its spinning. Mother drew in close, put her hand into her apron pocket and threw flour full into its face.

The dragon sneezed, blowing Mother over, and shook its head wildly and painfully. Giddy and blinded, it spun round and round, clawing at its eyes. I saw my chance in its blindness and confusion – and came in carefully, avoiding the flapping wings. One touch would knock my head off.

I came over it, and down. Then was on its back, as in a saddle, between two spines, just above the wing. The creature was too busy to realise I was there, clearing its eyes, getting over its giddiness. But it was coming to, levelling in the air, its flying less frantic.

All at once the dragon seemed to know I was there. It bucked like a horse, flipping its body up and down. I hung on for dear life. If I fell either the wings would smash me or the dragon would catch me and crunch me in an instant. I held tight with my knees, and clutched both arms round the spike in front of me as the creature's body writhed and contorted in its efforts to throw me off.

In a while, it gave up on that, perhaps to take a break and then begin again. But instead it flew up into the air. And I knew what was coming. I held on as the dragon pushed on higher, into the thinner, colder air, up in the clouds. Without warning, it did a u-turn, and dived. Out of the cloud we came, zooming faster and faster down to the ground. My stomach jumped into my chest, my eyes filled with water, and I held on with freezing hands as the dragon dropped, gathering speed each instant in its vertical dive. The wind scoured me, I threatened to fly off backwards, my arms stretched like cords.

But this was no suicide mission. The creature must slow or smash into the mountain. And slow it did, easing into the horizontal perhaps 100 feet above the surface. I could hear by its forced breathing how exhausted it was. Fifty tons of animal could not writhe and thrash and climb to the clouds without tiring. Gently it coasted, resting on the wind, renewing its energy for its next assault.

But this was my turn. I was over the wing, the animal flying as slowly as it could to stay in the air. There would not be a better time. I withdrew my knife from my belt. And choosing my moment, hacked at the sinew of the right wing. One chop, a quick second, and the sinew snapped like a taut rope. In an instant, the wing, which has been horizontal fell to the side. And the creature descended, no controlled dive this time: it plummeted like a stone dropped from a tower.

My intention was to fly off but I found myself dragged down in its wake. I crunched my toes to fly upwards, but the down draught was too strong. So I fell too, perhaps ten feet above the dragon, as out of control as it was.

And then it smashed to the ground, and the up draught propelled me up, way up, where my shoes finally took hold, and gently I lowered myself. The dragon was lying slumped out, blood pouring from its mouth in rivulets.

I landed. And Mother joined me.

Together, we walked around the creature. I prodded it with my knife here and there. But it was as lifeless as a trussed chicken.

'Cut its head off,' said Mother.

I looked at her aghast.

'No one will believe us,' she said, 'if we return with nothing.'

Mother left me to go down the mountain, while I had the butcher's job. The knife may have been sharp but a dragon's neck is thick and bony. I hacked and chopped and was covered in blood by the time it separated from the body.

By then, Mother had returned with a wheelbarrow. With difficulty we lifted the head, put it in the wheelbarrow, and set off down the mountain with our gruesome load.

Our journey home was nothing like the one out. We were welcomed everywhere, cleaned up, given food and new clothes by grateful villagers. Yes they had suffered awfully, but it was over. We had the evidence. Mother and I were given a horse and cart to ride more comfortably back to our own village.

And there we were greeted with surprise. They had not expected to see us again. But the dragon's head made clear that we had completed our task. And we were feted as heroes. The villagers assisted us in rebuilding our cottage. And we were given money from the Mayor's funds to set up our bakery once more.

It seemed that life was returning to normal. But it was not long before I realised that things had been set afoot, that would change me completely. And I was no more in charge than a leaf blown from a tree.

Chapter 2

The village was busy the morning the man came, with the banging and hammering of rebuilding. Ours had been the first house to be rebuilt, part of our reward from the villagers. Besides, everyone said, with all the work to be done – a bakery was essential. Then we began on the others. Work was good for the village. It gave people a reason to get up in the morning and stopped them dwelling on the casualties. Even so, at lunchtime, when labour stopped, there was a deal of sadness. A man might wander off to sit on his own, with tears streaming down his face. And no one needed to ask why.

When I wasn't helping Mother in the bakery, I worked with the others. It was everyone together, remaking the village. We would complete a house and move on to the next. Of course men and women couldn't be there all the time as they had their own jobs to do, but any spare time they had was taken up by building. Or cooking for the crew. I wasn't much good at carpentry when I first started but I improved over the weeks. And learnt to saw quickly and straight. I loved being up the ladders and on the roofs, hammering in nails with my shirt off. And I remember thinking that, for a trade, maybe carpentry is better than being a baker.

You might wonder why I needed a ladder when I had my flying shoes. I came quickly to realise they weren't everyday things. If I showed off in them, then someone would steal them. Also I'd lose all element of surprise. Better to wait until I needed them.

We were finishing off the Williams' house when the man came. I was helping to fix a door, when Josie ran over. She said I must go home at once as there was someone important to see me.

'Me? You sure?' I said in surprise.

'Quick, quick!' she said. 'He says he can't stay long.'

So I ran home, putting my shirt on the while.

Our door was wide open. It always is, the back door too, as the heat from the oven could make Jack Frost sweat. Besides, an open door is inviting to customers. Outside a black horse was tied up, and I wondered what this was about. A man on horseback to see me? I straightened myself up and wished I could wash, but quick the word was – so I'd best see who it was.

Inside, the man was sitting at a small table, his feet sprawled out so I nearly tripped over his boots. He was wearing green livery, with red piping and silver buttons. His soft green hat was on the table by a leather pouch, along with a mug of beer and a chunk of bread he was munching. Mother was working behind the counter, pounding a large slab of dough on the baking table.

'This the boy?' said the man.

He had curly brown hair and was quite young, only a few years older than me. I wondered how he could get such an important job at his age, even though I didn't know what the job was then – but the uniform was so smart, it had to be important. And the way he was lounging about the shop as if he owned the place…

'Yes,' said Mother. 'That's my son.'

She was tight-lipped and frowning. I could understand why. A man like this could bring good news or bad.

The man opened the pouch and took out a parchment letter with a red wax seal. He handed it to me. My name was on the front in thick and thin, curly writing, *Will Baker Esquire*, with a flourish underneath.

'I didn't know I was an esquire,' I said.

The man laughed. He said, 'That's what you are if you are nothing else.'

I was still holding it, admiring the writing and the bright red seal.

'You can open it,' he said.

I looked to Mother. I didn't want to break that beautiful seal.

'Open it, Will,' she said, her lip trembling.

So I did. The seal cracked. And there was a letter inside. I read it out:

To Will Baker

The King has heard of your heroism and commands you come to the palace post haste.

It was signed something like Orex. But the signature was done in a rush, not like the rest of the letter which was beautifully written like the writing on the envelope.

When I scratched my head over the signature, the man took the letter from me.

'That's the King's signature,' he said. 'Orex. Stands for Oliver rex. King Oliver.'

'He writes short letters,' said Mother.

'He's busy with affairs of state,' said the Messenger, for I realised then what he was. 'And you'd better get yourself ready, young man.'

'Am I coming with you?' I said.

The Messenger rolled his eyes. 'You are most surely not. I've got six other letters to deliver.' He threw back the beer and picked up the lump of bread and stuffed it in his pocket.

'How do I get to the palace?' I said.

'Any way you fancy,' he said. And put on his hat and was gone.

Chapter 3

What could the King want with me? A reward perhaps, for killing the dragon. Maybe the Mayor had sent word to him. It turned out that he hadn't, but the story had got out. Dragons are not killed that often, it's mostly they who do the killing – but when one is, everyone soon knows about it.

I was famous!

And was given lots of advice. The Mayor told me to bow and say Your Majesty, and only speak when I was spoken to.

'Pick no fights,' he said, 'and be a credit to the village.'

Mother packed food for me: buns, cheese and a cake or two. She gave me a pound, all in pennies, as she said it would be easier to spend and I'd be less likely to be robbed.

The next day, I rose in the misty morning, the sun hardly above the horizon. I'd not been able to sleep, I was so excited. Mum said I should leave early as then there'd be no more fussing. And I agreed; I'd had enough advice to fill a barrel.

She kissed me on the cheek, told me not to be a nuisance.

'And keep your flying till you really need it.'

I said I would. Who knew what could happen? And if everyone knew I could fly – then where's the wonder in that? I would walk to the palace, like a baker's boy should.

I set off.

There was hardly anyone up as I went through the village. I wanted to sing 'I'm going to see the King', but been told often enough not to boast, though I was bursting to. No one in our village had ever been called to the King. A few had seen him in his carriage as he came through here and there. But that's not the same as being called to see him. Getting a special letter with a red seal. Having a messenger come just for you.

I had my food in a shoulder bag and a blanket, rolled and tied across my back. Inside were clean clothes. The walk, I was told, would take four or five days, and I could stay in inns, for a pound was enough for that, or I could sleep in the hedgerow, depending where I was. It was all fine by me. I was going to meet the King.

The road to take was no problem. I had to stay on the road that ran through our village until it met the main droving trail which lead straight to the palace. The weather was mild, and everyone who saw me must have thought me simple as I was beaming as I walked, for I was so proud of my mission.

I tramped all morning without trouble and stopped to eat by a stream.

There I saw a man sitting on a rock a few yards away.

'Good morning,' I said.

But he did not look up, intent on what he was doing, something on the rock which I could not see. He was portly and possibly a priest as he wore the itchy brown cassock that some of them wore, but what made me doubt it was the fact that he was so scruffy. If cleanliness was next to Godliness, then this man was best friend to the devil. He was bald but had a tatty beard and at most three blackened teeth. He twisted his body, and I could then see that on the flattened table top of the rock, he was playing with three half walnut shells. I knew this trick; there was a pea under one of them, and you had to find it. I had seen it when the fair came to our village, and a man there had cleaned out half the village before the Mayor had him drummed out. But this man, priest or not, plainly wasn't much good. I watched him practising, putting the pea under one shell and shuffling them around. And I guessed right every time.

I thought I could easily win here.

I packed my food away and approached him.

'Can I play?' I said.

He looked up at me. His eyes were dark with heavy, tired rings round them.

The man didn't speak but nodded.

He put a pea under one of his walnut shells in plain view. He then shuffled the shells about rapidly, but it was quite easy to follow. He stopped.

'Which one?'

I bet ten pence, and pointed. And won. And another. And won again. I put all my winnings on the next. And won. This was too easy; there must be a trick coming. He was trying to lure me in. But try as I might, I couldn't lose. I must have had five pounds piled in front of me in silver and copper. It got to the point where I wanted to lose. I felt sorry for the man. But I found I couldn't lose. I began to realise that the man was cheating to lose. Whatever shell I picked, if the pea wasn't there already, he was somehow slipping it under.

I wanted to leave. I stood up, but the man grasped my wrist and pulled me back down.

'Play,' he said.

And so we played on. And in dreadful monotony I won and won. Not a single game did I lose, try as I might. At last he rose and pulled out his pocket lining. He smiled a gap-toothed smile.

'All gone.'

He held out the shells to me. He still owed me some small amount, twenty pence or something, I'd stopped counting.

'Yours.'

I waved my hands. 'No, it's alright. I don't want them.'

'I owe you,' he shouted.

'It's alright,' I said, frightened by his anger.

'Take them.'

And so I took them. I swear I didn't want them. I had his money, I hadn't wanted all that either. Just a bit more. Not every penny.

'Have some money,' I said. And offered a handful of change.

At which the man shook his head violently, turned and ran away as fast as he could. Down the road I watched him, not once did he look back, until at last he disappeared over the brow of a hill.

I collected up the money and put it in my pockets. I felt quite weighed down. I rose to leave.

And found I couldn't.

I could stand up but I couldn't take a step. It was as if my legs were nailed to the ground. I pulled and I tore, but my legs would not walk. In futility I yelled after the man, but he was long gone. Clearly I was bound in the spell which he had escaped from.

I sat back. I had plenty of time to think about it. To work out what had happened. There was some strange magic here. The man had been trapped, and had been able to escape by losing all his money, and finally giving me the shells. I was now the victim and the man, for all I knew, was running still. Free, but who knows how long he'd been stuck here?

I would have to escape the same way. Find my victim, and pass on cash and shells. Or be stuck here forever.

I began feverishly to practise the three shells game. After a lot of messing about, I found the best thing to do was to get the pea out at once. Show the pea, put the shell slowly over it, snaffle it out with my little finger and hold it, ready to sneak it under one of the others.

The road was a quiet one. It hadn't yet joined the main droving trail. And so it was a while before anyone came. I had plenty of time to practise.

At long last, there came a man pushing a wheelbarrow full of turnips. He stopped by the stream to drink. And I began playing the game to get his attention. Once it starts, it's pretty difficult not to watch, and I had him watching almost at once.

'That one,' he said.

I lifted the shell. He was right. I made sure of it.

We played again. He was right once more.

'For a penny,' I said.

We played for a penny and he won. And then more money, slowly my pockets becoming lighter and his pile increasing.

At one point he scratched his bald head. 'I'm either very good or you are very bad.'

'You're very good,' I said. 'The best I have ever played with.'

And so we played on. I wished he'd go for one big stake, so the game would be over, but he had a farmer's caution and played for a maximum of ten pence, and often five or one, as if expecting to lose. Except he always won.

He stopped, looked at his pile of cash and said, 'What will your mother say when you come home with no money?'

I was a bit flustered, not expecting the question, and didn't know what to say. So he repeated it.

At last I said, 'I have no mother, sir. I am an orphan.'

'Oh you poor boy,' he said. 'I can't take any more of your money. In fact have this back.'

And he pushed half his pile to me.

'I don't want it,' I cried.

'Neither do I.'

And he took the handles of the wheelbarrow and was off.

'Poor boy, poor boy,' he called back to me.

'Please play!' I yelled after him.

But he took no notice, and was soon gone.

I went back to practising shuffling the shells. It is a most boring game, and I was feeling desperate. I had set off to see the King, and here I was stuck by the stream, waiting to trick people. I was miserable. I must do better with the next one.

At last came a tall thin man. The sun was shining, still high in the sky, and he stopped at the stream to drink and fill his water bottle. I began shuffling my walnut shells. And he stopped to watch.

'That one,' he said.

He was of course right. He would never be wrong. And so we played on, eventually getting into playing for money. He won of course. But oh, he took his time. He had a great bush of ginger hair and he would muss it up as he thought. This one, that one? And all the time I was thinking – just pick one and I'll slip it under whichever you choose. But no, he wanted to work it out. And to praise himself for doing it.

'I'm a right clever 'un,' he said as he won once more.

'Oh you surely are,' I said. 'I don't know how you do it.'

And so we played on.

He wasn't very bright, but even he began to wonder why he won every time.

At last he said to me, 'What will your mother say when you come home with no money?'

Well I knew the wrong answer to this question.

So I said instead, 'My mother is rich, sir. And she gives me lots of money to play with.'

He looked me up and down and said, 'That's not a rich boy's coat. Nor a rich boy's trousers.'

'I leave my good clothes at home,' I said. 'I like to pretend I'm poor.'

He scratched his ginger thatch, looking at me, looking at the money. 'The rich don't give their money away.' He stared me hard in the eye. 'This is stolen money – isn't it?' And then in some alarm added, 'You stole it from your poor mummy.'

'I never did, sir,' I declared.

'I'm not going to hang for taking a poor widow's cash.'

And he pushed it all back at me. And was off.

'Go home,' he yelled as he strode away down the road. 'Tell her you are sorry.'

And I all but wept. We had played for an hour or more. And I had got nowhere, for every penny he had given me back. How was I going to get away from here? The sun was getting lower in the sky. In a few hours it would be dark. I ate a little, I could just reach the water of the stream if I lay flat out. And I thought of the answer to the question – what will your mother say when you come home with no money? I couldn't be an orphan, that just got me sympathy. I couldn't be a rich boy, that wasn't believed. I tried quite a few answers but none struck me as very good. The best I could come up with was: *I dug it up, sir, in a field. So she doesn't know I have it. And if I come home with no money, then that's no more than I left with.*

I simply had to leave this rock and steam. I would be late for the King. My food was getting low – I'd starve to death. I had to lose my money and get away. Time seem to have halted, as I watched the road for any passer-by, someone eager to win my cash. And take my walnut shells.

But my next visitor did not give me the opportunity, either to lose my money or to try out my new answer. He was not a gambler or the questioning sort.

It was a bear.

The creature came trundling down the road quite slowly, as his legs were linked together by a short chain no longer than my arm. Plainly he had escaped. I'd always felt sorry for dancing bears, laughed at by the crowd, taunted by their master as they danced for pennies. But I had no sympathy for this one.

His brown fur was patchy, the arms hefty and strong, the legs short and thick. Evidently pleased to see me, he growled, and I noted he had a full set of teeth. I wondered when he had last eaten. Perhaps he was wondering the same as he approached me, the chain clinking as he strode.

I jumped, I tugged – frantic to get away. But pull as I might I was stuck by the rock. I tried taking my shoes off, but I couldn't. It was as if an iron rod went from the ground, through my shoes and up my legs. And every time, I looked up, the animal was closer, arms pawing the air, its pace hobbled by the chain – but still arriving too soon.

There was nothing I could do. I was fastened. A prisoner to this rock. An easy victim to a big brown bear.

But first it went for the stream and filled itself. I watched it bent over and slurping, that huge back, as wide as a door, drinking before dinner.

And when it had had enough, the bear turned to me.

'Pretty bear,' I said in as gentle a voice as I could muster. 'You are so strong and handsome. Pretty bear...'

And those were the last words I spoke. For the bear grasped me round the chest in both arms, in such a hug I could hardly breathe. It tugged at me, puzzled, for I was stuck. And so it tugged harder. And still I would not give, though my legs threatened to separate from my feet. So it pulled even more, as if at one end of a tug of war, the rock the other and me the rope. But I was so crushed in its grip, I could not even moan, as it yanked and growled, perhaps believing there was another bear underground competing to have me.

I feared it might be half each.

But then I tore away. Even the magic could not hold me against the strength of the brute. The bear staggered backwards, releasing me for an instant. I scrunched my toes. And I was flying.

Up into the clear blue sky. Leaving the bear down below, its arms raised to heaven as it growled, sorry it had not at once bitten my head off.

My money was gone, my blanket and spare clothes were gone. But I was free, and going to stay free. And so I flew off.

Chapter 4

A little later I thought of going back for my money and clothes. There was my knife too. The bear would have left – surely? But suppose I became trapped again? No, better away and free. I could imagine though the next traveller arriving, pocketing the pile of coins, picking up the walnut shells... And the story beginning again.

But it would not be me.

I was walking once again. Lighter, too light. No food, no change of clothes, no blanket to sleep in the hedgerow. And no money for an inn.

Where was I going to stay the night?

It wasn't yet dark but the sun was low, the heat ebbing from it. The sky was clear and I knew, once the sun set, it would grow cold. I had to find somewhere quickly.

Up ahead was a cottage. I would try it.

The dwelling had two storeys with white walls and a thatched roof. Whoever owned it was quite well off. Smoke was coming from the chimney. Someone was in. I approached, went through the low garden gate and knocked on the stout door.

I crossed my fingers. This cottage was isolated. It could well be dark before I found another. I rehearsed my words.

The door was opened by the most beautiful girl I had ever seen. Every word I'd thought out flew from me. I could not take my eyes off her. Her hair was black and fell below her shoulders, her skin pale and smooth, her brown eyes catching the low sun. I tried to speak, but could not say a word. She was about my height, and so her face was full on mine, like the sun to the full moon.

She smiled at me, seeing my helplessness.

'Can I help you?' she said in the gentlest of voices.

I nodded. I could just manage that.

She waited. I had to try.

In a stuttery voice, I said, 'I've had bad luck. Lost my money. Can I work for a bed and food?'

She pursed her lips thoughtfully, then said, 'I'll ask Mother.'

And went away, leaving the door slightly ajar, and me trembling still.

I could hear voices within, but not make them out. Soon she came back.

'Can you chop wood?'

'Yes,' I said, and that was true enough, for at home I chopped wood every day to feed our oven. But would have said yes to anything she asked.

She stepped out of the cottage and beckoned me to follow. I did so, and this was the first time I noted what she wore, having been held totally by her face. Her skirt was black and long, down to her ankles and small shoes. She wore a white blouse, the sleeves short and bunched, the collar loose and lacy. Strange clothes I might have thought for a country girl, but I was not thinking.

The girl took me to the side of the cottage. And there was a pile of logs with an axe leaning against it.

'Chop us some firewood,' she said, 'and there'll be supper and a bed for you.'

I was eager to please and took up the axe. And began chopping at the wood. Once she saw that I knew what I was doing she left me. So I breathed easier. I had food coming and was promised a bed. My luck was in.

And I wondered about the girl. She was about my age. Did she have a boy friend? Had she been swayed by the way I handled the axe?

I would chop so much – and, I day-dreamed, perhaps be asked to stay on a few days. So I worked hard, cleaving the logs, wanting to impress her by the time she came back.

But eager as I was, quite soon I needed a break, and when I did so saw a cat watching me. The animal was totally black, except for the green of its eyes and pink within its ears. Whiskers twitching, it stood on all fours facing me, its long tail curled in a rising S.

The cat hissed, 'Take your chance, boy, and get away from here.'

I was a little thrown by a speaking cat, but didn't like its tone.

'I'll stay, thank you,' I said. 'I've a meal coming. And a bed for the night.'

The cat turned away.

'You've been warned,' it hissed. And began to stroll away, then turned its head back. 'Don't eat the food.'

And walked off.

A talking cat was a surprise, but not the greatest one. Hadn't I seen dragons and been held to a rock by magic? As for its warning, it could not compete with the beauty of the girl's eyes. I continued chopping wood, wanting only to see her again.

After a time, she came out again, as lovely as ever.

'You have done well,' she said looking at the pile of wood I'd chopped. 'Supper is nearly ready. You might like to wash.'

'Yes,' I said, the first word I'd said to her in ages.

My conversation needed to improve if I were to get any further.

She went off and came back with a bowl of water, a bar of soap and a towel over her shoulder. She stayed while I washed. And I was pleased to wash off the grime: the dust of the trail and the sweat of chopping wood.

When I had done, she threw the dirty water into the hedgerow and I followed her round the house and in through the backdoor. The sun was setting and there was a lamp already lit in the window of the room we entered.

Cooking over a fire was an old woman. She was bent over, her head tied in a red scarf with wisps of grey hair escaping from the front. Her face was wrinkled, her eyes deep set. And when she smiled at me, it was through a few broken teeth.

'My mother,' said the girl.

I was amazed at the age difference, thinking perhaps grandmother.

'Pleased to meet you, young man,' said the old woman, examining me closely. Her bony fingers were stirring the pot with the ladle.

'And I you,' I said, but didn't feel that way at all.

It was as if I had woken from a deep sleep. I didn't know these people. And the old woman was so old, so much more so than my mother. I recalled the warning of the cat who even now was sleeping on the hearth. And when I looked at the girl, for an instant she seemed older, or was it the effect of the light – for the years seemed to wash off when she shook her head, but straightaway she was as she had been.

We sat at the table. There was bread before us, and stew to be served up. I thought to myself I must not eat the stew. The bread would likely be safe enough. But how could I get out of eating further?

The old woman ladled out three bowls and sat down herself. I munched bread for a while as if waiting for the stew to cool.

'Have you come far, young man?' asked the old woman.

I told her of my village.

'He's very good at chopping wood,' said the girl.

And once more looking at her, the first glimpse had her older for an instant. Than rapidly washed off to her customary youth and beauty. I realised it only happened when I caught her quickly. My eyes it seemed then made her my age. If I was ten years older – would she be too? How old was she really? If the old woman was her mother…

'Eat up,' said the old woman.

I took a sip. It was beautiful broth. I could easily sup this bowl and more. And I dearly wanted to. The food I had taken from home I had left behind. And since then I had been walking and chopping wood.

Surely a little more wouldn't hurt?

There was a scratching at my foot. I looked down and there was the cat looking up at me. Within its paws was an empty bowl. I stretched down, seemingly to scratch my leg, and lifted the bowl into my lap.

I took another sip of soup, and oh it was delicious, but resolved I would have no more of it. The girl was turning the lamp up, the old woman was dipping bread into her broth. And I switched bowls. Then made out to be wiping the last of the broth with my bread.

'Delicious,' I said.

The old woman looked at me and the bowl, wide eyed.

'You eat quickly,' she said.

'I was hungry.'

She beamed at me, her five-toothed smile. 'Then have some more.'

I waved her offer away. 'Oh please no, that was plenty.'

'Oh I'm sure you want some more,' said the girl. 'Really you do.' She turned to her mother. 'He's just being polite.'

How could I refuse?

In fact I was not given the opportunity as the old woman took my bowl and went to the pot over the fire and filled the bowl. But then for an instant turned her back on me. And I thought, she's putting something else in, I swear it. The old woman turned round holding the steaming bowl, came round the table and put it before me.

'I'll let it cool,' I said.

The old lady nodded. Then said, 'Perhaps you'd like to stay a few days, young man. Be company for Jemima.'

At which the girl nodded.

The invitation that I had wished for had come. But it was all wrong. There was something sinister here. I had to leave as soon as I could. But not now, I had to pretend I suspected nothing. What was I to do with the soup?

I let it cool some more. Ate bread. Told them about my visit to the King which made the two of them smile at each other. And then smile at me. As if I was soft-headed and they knew something I didn't.

And surely they did.

I went to get more bread from the board and deliberately tipped over my bowl. It fell off the table onto the floor. I stood up and the bowl in my lap went too. There on the floor was a puddle of broth, and the debris of two broken bowls. And looking up at me was the cat with the largest piece of china in its jaw. It ran off.

'I am so sorry,' I cried out.

My cry was not fabricated. The soup was hot, and had soaked through. At once there was a fussing all around me. I was wiped and the broken china taken away. And I began to realise what the cat had done. Two broken bowls would have been obvious, but with a big piece taken, a lot less so. So they probably still thought I'd eaten the first bowl. It was a little while before we all settled down once more at the table.

'I am so tired,' I said.

I feigned weariness. And from the look they gave each other, I realised this was expected.

'It's been a long day,' said the girl gently. 'Let me take you to your room.'

I rose and she took a candle and led me up the stairs, then along the hallway to a room. She opened the door and handed me the candle.

'I'll call you for breakfast,' she said with a smile. Then added, 'Perhaps we could go for a walk tomorrow. I'll show you the farm.'

'I'd enjoy that,' I said.

She kissed me on the cheek. 'Sleep well.'

And she turned away, while I went into the room and closed the door.

The room was larger than I had expected. There was a wide window and on the sill I placed my candle. By one wall was a single bed, alongside it a large rug. A chair, a chest of drawers and quite an expanse of wooden floorboards. It was comfortable enough. But I knew I must not spend the night here.

I looked out of the window. It was dark outside. I opened the casement and looked down. I could drop that distance without much damage.

Suddenly the cat sprang in through the window.

'Thinking of dropping down there?' it hissed.

'Yes,' I said.

'Straight into quicksand,' the cat said.

I strained to see more clearly with the light of the candle.

'It doesn't look like it,' I said.

'Of course,' said the cat. 'What would be the point of that?'

'I've got flying shoes,' I said. 'I could fly away.'

The cat sniffed. 'You can't. Any magic you have, they have neutralised. You'd be straight in the quicksand.'

'What's going on in this house?' I cried.

'Sh!' hissed in the cat.

I repeated my question quietly.

The cat strolled about the room, sniffing here and there, in corners, along the edges, and then returned to me.

It said, 'The old woman is a witch. She's 960 years old, or thereabouts. Her daughter is 500 or so...'

'That's impossible.'

'Fat lot you know,' said the cat. 'Stroke my back.' I did so. 'Oh yes, that's nice.' It gave a squirm under my hand. 'Give my head a scratch... where was I?'

'Their age,' I said.

'To stay young, they make a potion from the blood of young people.'

'They mean to kill me?'

'Hundreds have slept in this room,' said the cat. 'None have woken up.'

I sank onto the bed.

'What must I do?'

'Don't sleep in the bed.'

I rose and sat in the chair.

'Don't sit in the chair.'

I jumped up and sat on the rug.

'Or on the rug.'

I got off and perched on the windowsill.

'That will do.'

'Can't I just leave now?' I said. 'Sneak downstairs and out.'

The cat shook its head. 'No. They'll see you. They have spells. You must wait – until it has happened. Then.'

'Why are you helping me?'

The cat hissed and shivered. 'The old woman scalded me. Her daughter locked me in the woodshed for three days. I vowed vengeance.'

'But you've witnessed all these other murders?'

The cat shrugged. 'What happens to human beings is nothing to do with me.'

It was curled round, licking its hind legs. I sat down on the floorboards, my knees held to my chest. 'So if they hadn't treated you so badly...'

'You would have drunk the broth,' added the cat helpfully. 'And now be fast asleep in the bed. And very soon...' the animal stopped. 'Listen. It's beginning.'

At first I could hear nothing, then a faint whirring beneath the floorboards.

'It's the mechanism,' said the cat.

We sat in silence, both on the floorboards, listening. The stub of candle was flickering, throwing shadows around the walls and reflecting off the window. It wasn't cold but I shivered.

The bed began to move, slowly at first. And I realised it wasn't the bed. It was bolted to the floorboards, and the boards were turning. As it came to the vertical position, facing me, the blanket and pillow slipped down into the hole, ending in a splash. The mattress was tied to the frame – so did not follow. But whoever was in the bed most surely would have.

And then the chair. Down it went through the floor, as if a giant hand had grabbed it by the legs and pulled it through. So quickly, that if I had been sitting on it, I would have gone with. And another splash.

Then the rug. It curled itself up like a giant leaf out to catch a caterpillar. Then rolled along like a log to the hole in the floorboards where the bed had been. And dropped in, like a child going down a slide. And splash.

'Now's the time,' hissed the cat. 'We must be quick.'

The animal raced to the door. I followed with the candle.

'They'll go down to the cellar to check,' it said. 'And we must go to the kitchen while they are away.'

I opened the door and followed the cat along the corridor to the stairs, stepping as quietly as I could. Down the stairs we went. At the bottom was the kitchen, the fire still burning. A door was wide open.

'They are in the cellar,' hissed the cat.

The animal went to a shelf of books and pointed out a large volume with its paw.

'That one.'

I took it down and opened it on the table.

'Not that page,' said the cat. I turned over a leaf. 'Not that. Or that.' I turned more pages and the cat pressed a paw on my hand. 'That'll do.'

The cat jumped to the floor and came back a few seconds later with a stick in its mouth. I removed it. It was hot in my hand, a bumpy twig with the bark removed.

'As soon as you hear them coming up,' said the cat, 'chant the words on the page and point the wand.'

'Will it work?'

'Let's hope so.'

And so we waited.

I could hear voices below. Quiet at first and then angry. The anger was clear enough. They had the bedclothes, the chair and the rug – but not me.

Footsteps were rushing up the cellar stairs.

I began to chant and had just finished when the old lady appeared, followed almost at once by her daughter. I pointed them both out with the wand.

And instantly they disappeared, like bubbles that had popped.

In their place were two bats flying about the room. They flapped about my head, striking me with their wings. I tried to protect myself with my arms.

'Burn the book,' hissed the cat.

I rushed the book to the fire. My movement maddened the bats and they thrashed at me. But I wasn't to be distracted. Once in front of the fire I opened the book wide and threw it in. Immediately it caught. The bats gave up on me and tried to pull it out the fire with their claws, but squealed at the heat. In and out the fire they went, desperate to rescue the book, but plainly it was too heavy and too hot.

'It's their only hope,' hissed the cat. 'Or they'll die as bats.'

'Let them,' I said.

Their squealing filled the room as they darted in and out of the flames. Their wings were smoking, there was a smell of burning flesh. Disturbed by one of the bats, a glowing log fell out of the fire onto the rug – which in turn began to catch.

'We must leave,' said the cat.

By the time I was at the door, the room was filling with smoke. We left the house together. I closed the door on the squealing bats, still attempting to draw the book from the fire, with leaping flames catching the floorboards and table.

The cat and I watched from a distance. Quickly the house caught flame, sparks leaping into the air and lighting the dark sky like a firework display. The windows broke and fire came through the roof. Inside was a fireball of red and yellow that I had to shield my eyes to look at. We were on the edge of the island of light but could get no closer because of the fierce heat.

Not that we wanted to.

Chapter 5

We did not stay long, but set off to be away from the house. Although it was night, the light from the house lit the way like a sunset at our backs. I tried not to turn back and look, but every so often I had to. Standing on a low hill, watching the fire, I thought of the people that had died to keep the witches young. I thought of the cat by my side, eyes glowing like hot coals, who had not been bothered.

'Cat,' I said when we were walking again, 'why are you coming with me?'

'I thought it was you coming with me.'

We were side by side, so I realised it could be either way.

'Do you know where you are going?'

'No,' said the cat. 'Do you?'

'No.'

Away, only away.

The glow from the cottage washed away as we increased our distance from it. Once over a hill, we could see it directly no longer, but as an orange light on the horizon at our backs, as if the sun had set an hour before.

We were going through woodland and began to climb. And climb. Up and up we went, the trees thinning out. I was aware how hungry I was. I had only eaten a little bread at the witches' supper. And was tired too. I had chopped wood, eaten a poor supper and not slept a wink. By now it must be the early hours, perhaps two in the morning.

The landscape had become rocky with no trees at all. The fireglow had gone. We'd been walking for perhaps two hours. The house would be burnt out, I thought. No fire could burn so fiercely for long. The book was ashes, the bats too. There would be a few charred and smoking timbers, scorched knives and pots and pans, to be seen in the morning light.

We stopped at a gurgling stream we could see in the starlight. The water was icy cold, but I had to drink. Cat drank too. I knew we had come the wrong way but was reluctant to go back, not in the direction of the cottage. I could fly but had no idea where I was, so what was the sense of that? I would wait until light.

We continued walking. I hardly know why, except that it was too chilly to sit about.

'Cat,' I said. 'Have you a name?'

'They just called me Cat.'

'I can't just call you Cat. That would be rude. I shall make up a name for you.'

'You're not making a name for me,' the cat hissed. 'It's *my* name. I shall make it up.'

'Well if you like,' I said, 'but usually names are given.'

'I am not a usual cat.'

'That's true. How did you learn to talk?'

'Don't all cats talk?'

'No, they don't.'

'Whyever not?'

'I don't know.'

'You don't know much. I can only talk to one person. You are privileged. No one else can understand me.'

'Why is that?'

'This is tedious. All these questions. Magic is the answer. Because I am a witch's cat. Now stop interrupting. Where was I? Oh yes, my name… In future

I am to be called… Let me think. Yes, I've got it. I am to be called Smart.'

'Smart?'

'Well I am smart aren't I?'

'Yes, you are.'

'Now we are both agreed, Smart I am.'

We were still climbing. There were flat sections and then steep sections. I would have liked to have sat down and rested – but it was cold. And as we climbed higher, colder still.

There were signs of first light. And then streaks of gold above mountain peaks. The sun at last appeared, a cold orange sun. I shivered. Where on earth where we going? There would be no food here.

But I was wrong.

We went up a rise and then down into a dip. And there was a sort of house. I say sort of because it didn't have a front wall and the roof was flat. It was wooden and had only the one room. Not a proper house really, a shelter of sorts, but I wondered why they had not made a fourth wall.

Within was a table and two chairs. On the table were two bowls of porridge. I was too hungry to consider whom it might belong to. And so took up a spoon and had a sip. The porridge was cold but not unpleasant, made with milk and sugared. I rapidly ate a bowl and Smart leapt on the table and lapped the other.

Whose breakfast had we taken? I wished we could leave some money in payment, except I was penniless. But oh, I needed that porridge.

There was straw in a corner. And having eaten, I dropped exhausted into it. It had been a long day and night. And there was at least some shelter here. Smart snuggled next to me. And we fell asleep.

I don't know how long I slept, but when I woke it was pitch dark. A chair had fallen on me waking me up. The floor was rocking as if at sea. I could see nothing but could feel Smart next to me, still asleep.

I had difficulty standing up as the movement threw me. Once up, in the darkness I felt about like a blind man. I moved the chair away. My hands felt the table. I came in closer and pushed at it with both hands. The table did not move. And I became worried. For it was not so very long ago, I had experienced other furniture attached to the floor.

The rocking made it difficult to walk. So I worked my way round the table, to what I believed was the front. I reached out. And there was now a fourth wall. But no door or window in it, which is why it was so dark. Plainly we were being taken somewhere. On the back of a wagon perhaps.

We were somebody's prisoner.

'Boy!' hissed the cat.

I could not see it at all.

'Yes, Smart.'

'What's going on here?'

'The wall's been put in,' I said. 'While we slept. We're trapped.'

I could feel Smart brushing my legs.

'We're moving,' said the cat.

'A wagon perhaps?'

'No,' said Smart. 'The motion doesn't feel like a horse. And I can't hear the wheels of a cart.'

I listened.

There was a regular crunching, which came after a lift, then a fall and the crunch which shook us every time. We seemed to be travelling quickly, in our up and down motion. Smart was right, this was not horse-drawn. I thought of the sea, but the crunch was not right. I gave up trying to stand, crawled under the table and made my way back to the straw. It was easier on the ground, though I was still shaken up every cycle.

Smart came back to join me.

'Who's got us? Where are we going?' the cat hissed.

I could not answer either question. But was not sure I wanted to. Whoever it was had trapped us deliberately. And was now taking us somewhere, with some purpose in mind. That was as far as I could reason.

Sleep was out. The jogging was making me sick. I heard Smart retch, and then I was doing it myself. And out came the porridge. More would have come, if it had been there – but I was empty. Even so, I retched on throughout that miserable, dark journey.

The first signal that something was about to change was when the bumping halted, began again but more slowly. Then there were voices. Very loud, but I did not know what they were saying; it was not our language. And laughter, then could it be? – children's voices. That made me more hopeful. Rapidly I changed my mind; you never knew with children, they could hug a rabbit or cook it over a fire.

The wall suddenly slid back. The light blinded me, after being in the dark for hours. The voices were deafening, as if my head was in a thundercloud. I put my hands over my ears. And then still not able to see, I was tumbling through the air.

And landed on a pile of straw.

There was silence. The fall had winded me. I was beginning to see again, blurry at first. There was straw all around me, a foot or so in depth. Smart lay nearby, also trying to make out where we now were. As my eyes began to get used to the light, I could see the room was large and had bars on all four sides. We were in some sort of prison. Then I looked up.

The roof too was barred, running across to meet the bars making up the walls. And through it, I saw two massive heads staring down. For an instant I thought they were masks but the eyes were blinking, and then I saw a huge hand come to one of the heads and scratch the hair. And then above them, higher up came a third head. They all had chestnut brown hair, though the higher head had streaks of grey. The faces were reddish and freckled. And they were smiling, the lower heads with gaps between their teeth.

I lay back on the straw, like a four legged thing turned over, gasping, barely able to move, looking up at the enormous faces. My heart was beating like a mill race. I thought, what do they want with us? I wanted to explore our cage further but was terrified by the beings above us.

They were, I guessed, a family. The large one was the mother, the one with grey in her hair. The other two, her children, a boy and a girl perhaps though it was difficult to be sure. In human terms, the loss of teeth suggested they were about six or seven years old. Except they weren't human.

I'd heard of giants. Who hasn't? But never seen them, though someone who came in our shop said he had, but Mother didn't believe him. I did now. I glanced about as I hadn't heard from Smart for some time. He was as still as I was, on all fours, staring upwards at the huge figures.

I thought, they want us to entertain them. Like a mouse in a box. And I thought of doing something to get them laughing. As laughter is always safer. But also thought that if we entertained them, they'd stay longer and want more from us. So I thought, do nothing; let them get bored.

So I simply lay back on the straw and watched them watching me. The children's hands were on the cage, great stubby fingers with bitten down nails. Their smiles had gone; I thought, this could be dangerous.

Then the talking began – like claps of thunder. I pushed fingers in my ears as the sound boomed through me and the wind of their voices blew through the straw. I felt my head would explode with it. A finger poked in through the bars. It was like a long loaf of bread, except it wiggled.

The mother pulled the youngsters away. More talking, as the heads went out of my vision, and the voices faded.

A crash came, making us tremble in the straw. A door closing, I thought.

We were alone.

For a while, we were unable to speak or move.

Then Smart whispered, 'I don't like this. Not one bit.'

And that got me into motion. We were alone but that was not likely to continue.

'Let's see where we are,' I said.

We walked around the cage. It was open apart from the bars on walls and ceiling, no shelter, with the floor covered in straw. In one corner was a barrel of water. Would that have to do for washing and drinking? Nearby was a tray of food: nuts and bits of apple going brown, weary carrot and celery. I was starving and ate.

'Try some,' I said to Smart.

The cat sniffed at it. 'I can't eat that muck.'

I was less fussy and hadn't eaten for many hours. And this would do. The fruit and vegetables were dried out, but edible. While I ate, Smart continued exploring. Something was puzzling me; the food and water, it was as if they were waiting for us.

'Come here,' ordered Smart.

I sighed. He was a bossy cat, and sometime I'd have to deal with it. Or get used to it. Smart was in a corner, sniffing about. I came over, and, as I approached, the smell made it obvious what it was. This was the toilet corner. Though it had been cleaned up and the straw was fresh.

'Recent,' said Smart sniffing.

'How recent?'

'A day or two.'

That fitted with the brown apple and shrivelled celery.

Smart was still sniffing in the corner.

'Two distinct poos,' he said. 'Two people.'

'Where are they now?'

'Not here,' said Smart.

He did have the habit of saying the obvious. But even the obvious was disturbing. I looked about for other evidence of earlier habitation. There were two wooden chairs close to each other, suggesting a last conversation – panicked whispers perhaps. And also a wheel, a little taller than I was. It was raised off the ground in a frame, and had ridges like small steps going round it. I stepped inside, though I knew what it was. I'd seen one made for a pet mouse. I walked within it and the wheel began to turn. I walked faster and the wheel speeded up, turning under my feet. So we had food, water, a toilet corner and an exercise wheel.

But what had happened to those who were here before?

Obvious questions sometimes have obvious answers. Either they were somewhere else. Or they were dead.

I stepped out of the wheel. Smart was climbing up the bars of the cage; the gaps were too narrow for him to get through. The bars didn't start at ground level but at about my shoulder height. There was a sort of wooden fence all the way round which the bars slotted into. I stood on a chair looked over it and saw a surface of polished wood. On it was a bin, about my height, with a handle and I realised it was a giant's mug. Also a huge book lying on its side with strange writing on the spine. After about 20 feet the wooden surface stopped. I couldn't see down, but beyond I could see a window. It was high as a church, going almost to the ceiling, with yellow curtains on both sides.

'There must be a way in to this cage,' said Smart.

He was back down on the ground looking about him. I stepped off the chair and joined him.

'They have to change the straw and put the food in,' he said.

And there it was, way up at the top of the cage, perhaps 20 feet above us. I scrunched my toes and took flight.

'Impressive,' said Smart.

I was up at the ceiling of the cage. The door was made of bars and hinged at one edge, the other clipped into place. I pushed at it, but it was too heavy for me to raise. At this height, though, I could see more of the room. Under the window, I could make out part of a bed. I knew it was a bed, because of a red pillow. The bed I judged to be thirty feet long or more as I could just make out the end of it. In the other direction was the door. I knew it was tall, but it was difficult to judge how tall as I had nothing to judge it against. Tall enough for giants to come through. So fifty feet perhaps.

Even as I watched, it swung open. I scrunched my toes and landed, not wanting to be seen flying. In a few moments, the boy's head appeared over us. He had a furtive manner I didn't like. As if he shouldn't be here. His big hands rested on the roof of the cage. I was standing in the middle of the straw, looking at him looking at me.

He disappeared for an instant. Then came back with a stick in his hand. I say stick for it was to him, but more like the size of an oar to me. He poked it through the bars and jabbed at me. It was so quick, I hadn't been expecting it. And I grabbed the stick to protect myself. Instantly he pulled it up, and I slammed against the ceiling bars and fell to the ground, utterly winded.

This made him laugh, deafening me as I tried to feel if I had broken anything in my fall. But I was only bruised. Then he began to prod at me again with the stick. I made sure not to grab it this time, instead dodging out of the way. I could see by the way his face was twisting that my tactics were making him angry. He prodded, I jumped away, it was easy enough as long as he poked the stick through the bars. But having no success, he opened the door. He could get his hand and arm in now. And jabbed at me rapidly. This was terrifying, as I had to jump away instantly or really be prodded by the stick which he was thrusting with quite a force. He wanted to hurt me.

With repeated jabbing, he backed me into a corner. When I tried to get out, he waved the stick around me. If I wasn't careful he could smack my head off. I could hear him chortling, not that I was watching, my full attention was on the stick and its movements. Confined in the corner, he was going to get me. And do me a lot of damage.

The stick came down, I jumped and it missed me by inches. It came again and caught my jacket which I had to tear away. I was going to be stuck like a pig any instant...

And then Smart sprung onto the boy's hand. The claws dug in and Smart bit. The boy howled and pulled his hand out, Smart jumped and fell to the straw. The boy was leaping about, sucking his hand which was dripping blood. And wailing like a defeated army.

There was going to be hell to pay.

The howling brought padding footsteps and voices. And I thought about the former occupants of this cage. If they had been tormented by the boy and then fought back... Well what did people do to pets that bit?

His sister and mother appeared. Mother looked at the boy's bleeding hand, Smart had taken quite a lump out of it, while the boy whimpered. Mother clenched her fists and gave us a murderous look. The girl appeared with a fork. I had no doubt what she was going to stab.

'Come on, Smart!'

Smart leapt on to my shoulders. I could feel his claws gripping through the fabric. Above us the boy was still bawling, while mother and daughter had twisted, angry faces. And a fork each.

'Hang on tight,' I yelled.

I scrunched my toes. And rose rapidly in the air, and through the open door. Up swiftly, between the threesome, who swung at me with flailing arms. But I rose above, too high for them.

The girl threw her fork. It flew past me tumbling, as large as a javelin. Mother was flapping a cloth at us. I flew by them, another fork whistled by. I stayed above arm level, keeping clear of Mother's swiping cloth.

And out the window.

When I looked back there were three angry heads above the windowsill, shouting after us.

Chapter 6

I flew for quite a few hours to get us off the mountain. I landed just before a roadway, busy with carts, people walking and men driving cattle and sheep. I didn't want to fly straight on to the road and attract attention. My ability to fly was best kept to ourselves. It had worked with the giants. And who knew when I would need to do it again?

So I landed on a track a little way off and we followed it down to the main road. And so we entered the traffic on a warm day, the road dry and dusty. There was no doubt where the way led, for already in sight, perhaps five miles away, was the castle. Seeing it high on a hill with seven pointed towers, flags flying and white stone walls, I thought of my appointment with the King. What was I to be offered? How would my life change?

I wanted to tell the drovers and the carters that I was to see the King. But they would have thought me mad, so I simply told it to myself. But as important as my mission was, I was hungry with not a penny in my pocket. There were quite a few hawkers by the roadside, mostly selling food. Smart was able to dart in and end up with a titbit, while I tried to think of the castle and my visit as we walked on. Surely they would feed me there. I had, after all, been invited by the King. And five miles shouldn't take more than a couple of hours. Except it proved to be more than five. For at the end of two hours, we didn't seem to be any closer.

'I'm starving,' I said to Smart.

'Grab some grub then.'

'Easy for you, but they'd see me.'

'Watch me and take your chance,' said Smart.

The cat approached a low table where there were steaming pies. A man in an apron stood behind it, in front of his fire and griddle.

'Get your fresh pies!' he yelled.

Smart came in and tried to pull a pie off his table. The man slapped at him with his long fork. Smart retreated but came back again. The man threw a log at the cat, who retreated but came again. The man, enraged, charged at Smart. And I grabbed and pocketed a pie.

I ate it further down the road, once out of sight of the pie man. And Smart joined me a little later.

'Want some?'

'Keep it,' said the cat. 'I can feed myself.'

Once I'd eaten, I was thirsty, but there were streams on the way. I knew on a busy road like this to drink upstream of the road. That's where the water was clean, not contaminated by sheep and cattle droppings.

We at last got to the castle.

There was a drawbridge across the moat with a guard on either side. And a man on the bridge, not a soldier, though wearing a green uniform. He was talking to people who wished to go into the castle. Smart and I approached him.

'What are you here for, young man?' he said.

'I've come to see the King.'

'Have you an appointment?' he said.

'Yes,' I said proudly. 'He is expecting me.'

'Good,' he said. 'Now go into the courtyard.' He pointed the way. 'There you'll see two queues. There's a really long one – ignore that. It's for petitioners. Join the short one, it's for appointments only.'

I thanked him and stepped through the gateway into the courtyard of the castle.

The courtyard was busy. A wagon was unloading straw at the stable. Another had barrels of beer being rolled off. The sound of a blacksmith's hammer echoed off the walls. And servants, or so I assumed they were, darted from tower to tower on their various businesses, while those more grandly dressed traversed slowly. I spotted the petitioners' queue at once. It was so long that it snaked around the courtyard wall for perhaps two thirds of the its length. I was glad not to be in that one, for surely it would take all day to get to the front.

The appointments' queue was a lot smaller which is why I had difficulty finding it. It was before a small doorway where a fat, bald man in the same green uniform as the man on the drawbridge sat at a table with a book. We joined the queue; and I thought, we won't be long here. And watched the weary people in the petitioners' queue. I couldn't even see the front of it. You'd have to be desperate to join that line. It didn't seem to be moving at all. While our queue was brisk – and in perhaps five minutes we were at the front.

'You have an appointment with the King?' said the man.

'Yes,' I said proudly, puffing out my chest.

'Name,' he said.

'Will Baker,' I said.

The man looked down his book, which I noted was a list of names, running his finger under each.

'No Will Baker,' he said. 'Next.'

'But I've been sent for,' I insisted. 'Look again.'

The man sighed. His face was round, and his jowls drooped like a bloodhound. He licked his finger and it went down the names again. Then he turned back a page and went down that list.

'There. Will Baker,' he said.

'I said I had an appointment,' I said smugly.

'That was two days ago,' said the man.

'I came as quickly as I could, but I had trouble with witches and giants…'

The man held a hand up. 'I can't be troubled with excuses. You should have been at the castle two days ago. It says so here. See, next to your name – it says cancelled. So that's that. You had an appointment, Master Will Baker.' He looked up from the book and smiled grimly at me. 'And now you don't.'

'But I've come all this way,' I said desperately. 'Please, sir. What can I do?'

'You'll have to join the petitioners' queue. Next.'

And I was ushered out the way.

I looked in horror at the other queue.

'Don't hang about,' said Smart. 'It'll only get longer.'

So I made my way to the end of the long queue. And like so many others slumped to the ground, resting my back against the castle wall. I hadn't expected fanfares and a banquet, but hadn't a messenger ordered me to the castle… I had only come because I'd been told to come.

Smart left me and went along the queue. About five minutes later he came back and I hadn't moved an inch further up.

'Nothing's happening,' he said. 'There's not even anyone at the desk.'

It became clear after about an hour why there was no one there. For then the man at the appointments' queue closed his book and made his way, in no hurry at all, to the front of our line. And I understood the way it worked. First the appointments were dealt with and then, and only then, the petitioners had their chance.

Except quite a few didn't. I suppose some must have got in. At least I hoped so. But there were men and women, heads down in misery, walking back from the front of the queue, where they hadn't got past the man with the book.

All day we queued, slowly moving forward. I was hungry but determined to get to the front. By mid afternoon I had moved on far enough so I could see the door and the man at the desk. A few he let past, most he sent back. Had I come all this way just to be sent home?

By late afternoon, there were about 20 in front of us. And then the man closed his book. He shouted, 'No more petitions until tomorrow.'

Everyone in the queue groaned.

The man left with his book. Two servants took his table inside, and the petitioners' door was closed. Guards came forward to clear us from the courtyard. And so the queue broke up, pushed out of the castle.

'Now what?' said Smart, once we were across the drawbridge.

'I have to get some food,' I said. 'And find somewhere for the night.' I shrugged helplessly, 'And come back tomorrow, I suppose.'

'You could be here for a year.'

'What choice do I have?'

There was an inn close by and the Innkeeper agreed that if I was potman for the evening – I could get food and sleep in the stable. But he wasn't going to feed me straight away.

'In case you run off,' he said.

So I collected mugs and when it was quieter helped wash them up in the scullery. I managed to snaffle a bit of left over bread. And, after a couple of hours, I was given some food, a stew with heaven knows what in it, bits of bone and gristle and I didn't want to know what else. And the bread was stale, the sort of stuff Mother gave to the pigman. But I had nothing else, so must take what I was given.

I worked till midnight, until at last I was dismissed and shown to the hayloft of the stable. I was so tired I dropped off immediately. Still groggy, I was woken in the morning by Smart.

'Better get to the castle,' he said, 'if you want a good place.'

I rushed along but, by the time I got to there, the line was as long as it was yesterday. All the queuing I had done then had been for nothing. I went down the front and said this was where I was when the door had closed last night. But no one was having it. And I had to go right to the back of the queue.

I slumped down depressed. If anything I was even further back. I watched the man with the book, dealing with the appointments. I could see the way it was going to go. By the end of the day, I'd be up to 20th or 30th in line, and then it would close.

'This is a waste of time,' I said.

Smart looked along the queue, then at the shorter appointments' line.

'I'll see what I can do,' he mused. 'Stay here.'

That was easy enough. I had nothing better to do. The man with the book was being brought breakfast, so even the appointments' queue, short as it was, had to wait. We watched him eat a lump of bread and cheese and drink his beer. He was in no hurry.

What did he care who came or went?

I closed my eyes, not wishing to watch him eating. I was hungry enough already. I hadn't had any breakfast and had no food for the day. Should I just go back to my village? I thought. Oh how dismal that would be. I'd have to lie. Say I saw the King and he said this, that and the other. They wouldn't know any difference. Mum would though. She always knows when I lie. But there was little point waiting here and never getting to the front of the queue.

Smart returned.

'Go to the appointments' queue,' he said. 'Say you have an appointment for today.'

'But I haven't.'

'Do what you are told,' he hissed. 'Now!'

I hardly know why I obeyed. Perhaps it was just the thought of coming back to the petitioners' queue day after day.

So I left my spot. It was quickly filled. Much good may it do you, I thought. And joined the short appointments' queue. The man had eaten his breakfast, but his mug of beer was still beside him, and he sipped it from time to time. There were only six in front of me. And in a few minutes it was my turn.

'Next.'

'I have an appointment with the King today.'

I was afraid he'd recognise me from yesterday but he hardly looked at me. He'd seen so many people.

'Name.'

'Will Baker.'

And then to my astonishment, he began to write my name on a piece of paper with a quill pen.

'Eleven o'clock audience, Will Baker,' he said to one of his servants.

Utterly bewildered, I was handed the piece of paper and a servant led me through the door. How had this come about – as I most certainly didn't have an appointment today? I was aware of Smart rubbing against my legs.

'I'm in,' I whispered. 'What did you do?'

The servant led me along the corridor to a large door. Five others were waiting outside. He took my piece of paper, went in. A little later he came out.

'Won't be long, Master Will Baker,' he said. 'You will be called.'

And left us.

I got down to Smart's level.

'What did you do?' I hissed.

'Did you see the man's book?'

'No,' I said.

'He's lost it,' said Smart. 'So anyone who comes and says they have an appointment, he has to take their word for it.'

'I wonder how he lost it,' I said. Or rather how Smart had managed it.

'That'll teach him to eat so slowly,' said the cat.

I thought lucky all the petitioners don't know the book was lost. But then who was going to tell them?

One by one those in front went in. The audiences with the King, it seemed, didn't take long. But they didn't come out this way. The signal that it was over, to us anyway, was when the servant opened the door from inside the hall and beckoned the next one in. I grew more nervous as I got closer to the door. I must bow, be very polite. Speak clearly. Then I was in front. Be polite, speak clearly, bow…

The door opened; the servant peered at his list.

'Master Will Baker?'

'That's me, sir.'

'You come in now.'

He held the door open for me, and I went in, took a stride or two forward. And then just stood there, overwhelmed by all the people, by the draperies, and the ornate designs on the walls and ceiling. At one end, along a purple carpet that went from the door, was the King on his throne, raised up on a low platform. Along the sides were finely dressed men and women. I thought, when do I bow? The servant came past me and I followed his actions. He walked slowly along the carpet; I followed. He stopped about four paces from the throne and bowed deeply. I did so too.

'Master Will Baker, Your Majesty.'

'Ah yes, the dragon slayer.'

The servant backed away, still bowing.

The King looked at me closely. My legs were trembling, I could hardly stand. Those keen eyes… He was quite an old man with long grey hair, coming down to the shoulders of his wine-coloured robe. A jewelled gold crown was on his head. His fingers were knobbly and covered with rings with large stones.

'You don't look like a dragon slayer,' he said.

'I am, Your Majesty.'

And I bowed again. I wasn't sure when you should. Was one bow at the beginning enough? Or should you do it every so often to remind the King he was the King?

'What proof do you have?' he said.

I had never thought to be asked this. And for a moment couldn't think at all.

At last I said, 'There is a huge body on the mountain top.'

The King raised his eyebrows. 'Better if you were to say, it is under the sea.'

The court laughed.

'Or swallowed up in a volcano.'

The court laughed again.

'Or maybe you ate it for your supper?'

More laughter. They were loving this. My hands were sweating, ears burning. I could see the courtiers out of the corner of my eye, almost collapsing with merriment. I was the silly country boy at court.

Suddenly I felt angry.

I waited until the laughter had died. Then said, 'Why did you send for me, Your Majesty?'

'I heard there was a dragon slayer in my kingdom. I thought he would be a knight ten feet tall.' He indicated Smart who was by my side. 'Is that your charger?'

The court could not control themselves.

Smart hissed.

'Stay,' I said quietly.

He was by my side, in readiness to pounce.

The King was rubbing his rotund belly, plainly enjoying himself.

'Dangerous animal you have there. Fitting for a dragon slayer.'

More laughter. I was the most fun they had had in weeks.

I wanted to put a stop to it.

'Have you a task for me, Your Majesty?'

The King rubbed his bearded chin. 'Suitable for a dragon slayer, with so mighty a beast. Hm.' He paused as if contemplating deeply. 'Some test of daring, a trial of strength and bravery, a match for the mightiest warrior of my kingdom...' He paused once more, to make sure all his courtiers were listening. 'As it happens, I do.'

'I am your servant, Your Majesty.'

'Then you must destroy the Spider of Yoot.'

A gasp went through the court.

'Very well, Your Majesty,' I bowed. And when I had risen said, 'And what is to be my reward, Your Majesty?'

The King gave me the broadest of smiles. 'Why, as is customary for such brave feats, on completion – you shall marry my daughter!'

Laughter.

'Thank you, Your Majesty.'

I backed away bowing, and kept bowing, wondering why everyone was in howls of laughter. What did they know that I didn't? The hair on the back of my neck bristled, my throat was dry – but I continued going backwards and bowing. And it wasn't until I bumped into some courtiers that I realised I had not been going in a straight line.

A servant pulled me by the sleeve.

'This way, sir.'

And I followed him from the court, the merriment ringing in my burning ears.

Chapter 7

I was taken out by a side door, along a corridor, and out into the light of the courtyard.

The servant turned to me. I noticed even he was smirking. I was no noble who would kick him up the backside or smack him round the head.

'Go to the armoury,' he said.

'Why?'

'You have a Royal Mission, Master Will Baker. You must be equipped.'

He bowed, still smirking and went back inside.

I rested against the castle wall. I was exhausted. Yes, I had met the King – and been made a fool of. They'd treated me like a country bumpkin.

'I wanted to claw the King's face,' hissed Smart.

'That would have got your head chopped off,' I said. 'And mine too.'

'I hate these people,' he said.

And I knew exactly what he meant. For I did too. Those who made you queue all day and sent you back with nothing. Or invited you into an audience with the King and laughed at you.

A young lady was approaching, wearing a long dress to her ankles.

She said, 'Master Will Baker?'

I had never been called Master so much. And never wished to be again.

'Yes,' I said, wondering whether to bow. Her hair was long and flowing, too long for a servant's. And the embroidery around the neck of her blue dress too ornate.

'Come with me, please.'

I followed. She hadn't smirked, and she'd said please. And she was rather pretty too. She walked across the courtyard to a tower. I looked to Smart but he shrugged. Of course she could be the head torturer's daughter. But I didn't believe it. There was no blood under her fingernails.

She went to the door of the tower. A guard standing at the door with an upright spear tipped his head at her.

'Ma'am.'

The way she just ignored him, I thought she must be somebody. He opened the door for her and held it open for me and Smart. We followed the woman up stone steps that curled round the inside, ringing to our footsteps. We came to a landing where there was a single large door. She held it open.

'Please, come in.'

I walked in cautiously to a magnificent room. Sunlight streamed in the window and brought out the colours of the curtains and tapestries. There was a large rug on the stone floor. And soft decorated chairs here and there. In a tall vase on a chest of drawers was a large bunch of flowers reflected back in an oval mirror with gold surrounds.

A young woman stood up from a sofa to greet us.

The woman who brought me said, 'This is Master Will Baker, Your Highness.'

I bowed now.

'Thank you, Marianne,' said the Princess. She turned to me. 'Please sit down, Master Will.'

'Thank you, Your Highness.'

I knew that much. Keep saying Your Highness. And when in doubt – bow.

I sat down. And she sat down too. Marianne sat a little way from us and I gathered she was the Princess' maid. So I was wrong then, a servant – but not one who scrubbed floors. Or maybe a Princess' maid isn't a servant. Or a top servant. Or a sort of paid friend. How would I know these things?

'I like your cat,' said the Princess.

I could see Smart had not made his mind up about her, although I had.

'Thank you, Your Highness.'

'And I wish to apologise for the behaviour of my father.' She was looking down at her hands. 'He can be a pig. He has no call to invite people in, then humiliate them.'

'I did not expect to be so treated,' I said, then added belatedly, 'Your Highness.'

'I was there,' she said.

I had not seen her, but then had not noted any other faces but the King's. The rest were a taunting rabble.

'I'm glad there was one person not laughing at me,' I said.

She looked up at me. 'I have brought you here, not simply to apologise, but to ask that you do not go on the mission.'

'But the King has ordered it,' I protested.

She sniffed and waved a hand. 'He has, but he has already forgotten. By now he's found someone else to laugh at.'

'How many times has he offered your hand today?' I said.

'It's his silly joke.'

I had not taken it as a joke. Nor did I now, but said nothing.

'The best thing to do,' she continued, 'is to go home. My father has forgotten you already and if he hasn't, then he hardly cares. When you don't return, he'll assume, if he assumes anything, that you have been killed by the Spider of Yoot.'

'What is the Spider of Yoot?'

She waved a hand dismissively. 'Oh, some terrible monster. I don't know why they don't just leave it alone. But off they go, these knights. And they never come back.' She sighed, then added, 'So if you just go home, and never come back, there we are. They'll add you to the list of victims. And you can do whatever you do.' She pursed her lips. 'What is it you do?'

I hardly knew what made me say it, but it was out before I could stop myself.

'I am a dragon slayer, Your Highness.'

She smiled. 'Then the Spider of Yoot is quite out of your line.'

'I was thinking of the reward, Your Highness.'

She shook her head. 'Please go home.'

'I can't.'

She sighed. 'Then I wish you well. But I doubt we'll meet again.'

She put out her hand. I didn't know what I was supposed to do with it. So I took it in mine and shook it. I found out later I should have gone on my knees and kissed it. But she smiled and didn't seem to mind.

'Thank you for your kind wishes, Your Highness. And I do hope we meet again.'

'And I hope so too, Master Will Baker.'

I wondered whether she meant that. Or it was simply good manners? Oh, she was so much more pleasant than her father. She had risen to her feet.

Marianne was holding the door open. And I left as if flying.

Chapter 8

Marianne took us down the stairs to the courtyard. And left us.

I looked back up to window in the tower, and was disappointed that the Princess was not standing there. But I couldn't help but think that if I succeeded I could marry her. It was unbelievable, but hadn't I just been speaking to a princess. Me – Will Baker! And it was only when I left, going over what I'd said, that I realised how many Your Highnesses I had left out.

But she didn't mind. That was the point. That was what melted me. She was thinking of me, my safety. And I was thinking of her. And she had said 'I hope so too' when I said I hope we meet again.

'Take that silly grin off your face,' said Smart.

'I'm in love,' I declared.

'Heaven help us,' said the cat. 'You heard her. Go home.'

'Where's the armoury?'

Once I looked about, it was obvious. There was a large shed next to the blacksmith's workshop. Outside it a man in a brown leather apron was cleaning swords. I crossed to him, feeling the importance of my mission. I might yet be a prince.

The armourer was burly as if he had once been a blacksmith, but had put on weight with his grey hairs. He was working on a table, wiping a sword with an oily cloth; another half a dozen lay next to him.

I said to him, 'I need weapons.'

He looked me up and down. Then he smirked.

'You must be Master Will Baker.'

I was back in the land of smirks, and hoped I had left there forever, but here was another native of the country. I wondered what he'd been told.

'I am,' I said.

'Going to kill the Spider of Yoot,' he scoffed.

'Yes,' and to stop any more of his remarks, added, 'let's start with a sword.'

He had a number before him. Good stout blades, any one of which would have done, but instead he went into his shed. I heard him rummaging around amongst the metal. He came out with a worn, rusty sword I wouldn't have used to chop butter in summer. The edge was chipped; it was so rusty that a good swing at something hefty and it would snap.

'That thing?' I said, aghast.

'I'm not wasting a good sword,' said the armourer. 'You're not coming back.'

'I am,' I said.

'Look, Master Will Baker, I've had a dozen in here. Big, strong knights. And to begin with I gave them the best weapons I had. Not one of them returned. So now this is it.'

'I'm not taking it.'

He shrugged. 'Suit yourself.'

'I'll take a knife.'

The armourer sighed and went back in to his shed. And came back a few minutes later with a rusty knife.

'You're making fun of me,' I retorted.

The man glared at me angrily, his hands pressing against the table, perhaps so they wouldn't press round my neck.

'I am trying to warn you, boy.' He suddenly softened. 'Please, go home. This mission isn't for you.'

I looked at the two rusty weapons upon his table. Why bother with the weight? But then saw the one I wanted. In a flash I had grabbed the knife from the armourer's belt.

He swung a fist at me. I ducked and stepped back, holding the knife at him.

'This blade will stick,' I said.

A vein was pumping in his thick neck. But I was angry enough to fight him. He glared at me. I stood my ground, knife to the fore.

Then he relaxed.

'You've a little more mettle than I took you for.' He waved his hand, 'Keep it.'

'Thank you,' I said, and put it in my belt. 'How do I get to Yoot?'

'Go see the Map Master.' He pointed out a tower. 'There.'

I thanked him and left. He returned to cleaning his swords. I knew I had done well getting his knife. The armourer's blade would be the sharpest.

The Map Master was an old man with white hair and a long beard. He was dressed in black robes to his feet, seated at a table whose surface was submerged in papers and scrolls. To get to him we had to wander through the books and scrolls discarded on the floor, some open – all maps. He did not look up as we picked our way to him. Somehow with all those papers about him, with a quill pen he was carefully drawing, a map I supposed, working by candlelight as it was quite dark in the room.

I stood before his table and waited for him to look up. Now I could see it was a sea serpent he was drawing on the edge of the paper.

When he didn't respond, I said, 'Sir, I am Will Baker. Come for a map to Yoot.'

Without looking up, he pointed out a rolled document on the table, tied up with a red ribbon. I picked it up. It had my name along the length.

'Thank you,' I said.

He grunted and pointed to the door. And so we left him.

Out in the courtyard, I opened the document. And it was a map from the castle to Yoot. Not very well done. I had the feeling he had done quite a few of these, and rushed this one off with more important work to do.

It was while I was looking at the map that the armourer called over.

'Still set on going, boy?'

'Yes,' I said, holding up the document. 'I've got my map.'

He shook his head. 'If you will be a fool, then go to the kitchen - over there - and get yourself some supplies.'

I thanked him.

'You might as well eat before you die.'

We went to the kitchen. Once again in the land of smirk, but I did not argue or talk back as I wanted food for the journey. And so loaded up with bread and cheese, an onion, and a fish for Smart, we set off.

Chapter 9

I was relieved to be away from the castle. No one to laugh at us in the cool morning air. It was breezy, that alive wind that blows through your hair and seems to come from all around. We walked a few miles on a country road through small villages, and then cut off into the hills. I was following the map, turning it in the direction of the path we were following.

We stopped to eat. And were impressed by the armourer's knife. I had to chop off a piece of fish for Smart, and the blade was as keen as any I had come across. Mother kept her knives sharp but none like as this. I had bread and cheese with a little onion. We were by a stream and so had plenty of water to wash down our meal.

'What's your plan?' said Smart, spitting out fish bones.

'Plan?' I said, slowly chewing the bread. It was good, nearly as good as we made at home.

'You have got one?' said Smart.

'Well...' I said and stopped.

'That's an impressive plan.'

'I was just going to say,' I said a little irritated, 'that we first take a look at the creature. And then...' I hesitated, 'then make a plan.'

'It might be difficult to make one without a head.'

'So what do you suggest?'

'Go home,' said the cat, licking the last of the flesh on the bones.

'If I go home,' I said, 'I'll be a baker all my life.'

'But a live one,' said Smart. 'Don't forget that.'

I was going to say something about the princess when I saw a shadow over us. I turned, and there was a stocky man in a tunic, with wiry hair and a grizzled beard. He had a blanket over his shoulder and in his hands he carried a rope.

Suddenly he yelled, 'Surround and bind!'

And the rope whipped out of his hand. It wrapped round me and Smart. Its length stretching as it curled about and pulled tighter, pressing my arms to my side, and then running round my ankles. The rope then gave a tug and we fell to the ground like a rolled up rug.

'Good afternoon, my friends,' said the man. 'Let's see what you've got here.'

He rummaged through our meal and the other food. My knife was lying nearby.

'Good blade. I'll borrow that,' he said, 'and that bag. I'm sure you won't miss them.'

He gathered up the food, put it into the bag I had carried, slipped the knife into his belt. I didn't say a word, plainly the man was robbing us – and we were totally at his mercy. Smart was bound tight against me. I could feel his bristled fury. I hoped he would say nothing. The man could so easily cut our throats.

When he had everything, the man slung our bag over his shoulder.

It was then Smart hissed, bursting out like steam from a lid.

The man walked up and kicked him. The force of it going right through Smart and into my ribs. Smart hissed again. And the man kicked him again. I wanted to shout 'Shut up' to Smart. I could feel a trickle of blood. Mine or the cat's – I didn't know.

This subdued Smart. And satisfied, the man walked off. About fifty yards away he turned round.

He yelled, 'Unbind and Return!'

The rope whirled about us, twisting and curling – until we were out of its coils. Then it flew through the air, shrinking all the time, straight to the hand of its master. He twisted it round his arm and walked on, having no fear of us.

And well he might not, for it was Smart that was bleeding, the blood soaking through the fur in his forehead. I took him down to the stream and washed the wound. He squealed with the pain of the cold water.

'I'll get him,' snarled Smart. 'No one does that to me.'

'He'll just tie us up again,' I said. 'And cut our throats this time.'

'Not if we wait until dark,' said Smart.

And so we followed the man through the hills, keeping far enough back not to be seen. All day we followed, watching him eat our food, hearing his tuneless song, as we hid behind rocks to stay out of sight.

As it began to grow dark, the man collected wood for a fire. He lit it and put the fish on a stick and began to roast it over the flames. The smell wafted through to us. We were both hungry now, having gone the rest of the day without eating. But we did nothing until it was totally dark and the only light on the hillside the man's fire.

It was then Smart set off.

I lost him almost at once, a black cat on a black night. Nor could I hear his tread as he made for the man at the campfire. I crept in closer, the man was eating the fish; I knew this would make Smart angrier – if that were possible. I stopped behind a rock, and caught a glimpse of Smart just back from the fire: a glint of the eyes, a flash of the tail. Then gone.

And I waited.

At last the cat came back to me, the rope in his teeth. The man was still eating fish. We crept in. Then I stood up, the rope in my hand, and shouted:

'Surround and bind!'

The rope flew out of my hand. The man had dropped the fish and was running, but the rope flew after him, like an eagle after a sparrow. It spun round his ankles pulling him to the floor, then round and round his body, trussing him up like a calf going to market.

Smart and I went to the fire where he attacked the remains of the fish. I had bread and cheese and warmed myself at the flames. My knife was on the ground where the man had left it. I thrust it into my belt. The man, some way off, was groaning on the hard ground but we ignored him as we ate.

Once we'd eaten, we settled down for sleep. The man had a blanket which I wrapped myself in. Smart lay by the fire.

The man yelled out, 'I'm frozen, the rope's too tight. Let me free. I'll give you anything.'

We didn't bother to reply. We had everything he had anyway, and he was best tied up. Besides, if he was cold – he was asking the wrong people for sympathy.

We woke at first light. We had a little to eat and then I packed the food. Then I went over to the man who was a pathetic heap. His ankles were bound, legs tied together, a coil was round his chest pinning his arms to his side, and the rope ended having bound his hands behind his back. I was impressed; he was rather a neat parcel. And it was plain to see he'd had a terrible night; it would be impossible to get comfortable tied like that. There were rope burns on his hands which were red and puffy. His face was covered in dust where he'd been rolling around trying to untie himself or simply to ease his pains.

'Untie me, kind sir,' he pleaded.

'Why should I?'

'For mercy's sake,' he said.

'You took everything we had,' I said. 'You're best tied up.'

I didn't mean to leave him like that, as unless anyone came he would surely die, but a little longer to teach him a lesson.

'If I tell you how the rope works,' he groaned, 'will you let me go?'

'I know how the rope works,' I said.

'You don't know it all.'

'Tell me,' I said. 'And I'll let you go.'

'You know 'Surround and Bind',' he said trying to wriggle off his hands. 'And the instruction to release: 'Unbind and Return.'

'Of course.'

He'd have to do better than that.

'And you know, it only works for a person, free and in possession of the rope?'

I'd guessed that, otherwise the man could have freed himself.

'What else can it do?' I said impatiently.

'Say 'Climb and Bind' and it will tie itself to the top of a tree or a cliff – and hang down for you to climb up. If you need to cross a chasm – you must say 'Over and Bind'. And it will tie itself to the other side, leaving the end for you to swing across.'

'And 'Unbind and Return' will release it?'

'Always.'

'How far can I be away – for it to hear me?'

'About a mile or so.'

'Then we'll try it.'

Smart and I set off.

'Come back, kind sir,' he called struggling in the thongs.

'I will not,' I said. 'But we'll release you in a mile.'

And so we walked, ignoring his cries. We knew better than to release him too early. For, if we could follow him – then he could follow us. We needed distance. Smart and I climbed a hill, went along a ridge and down into a valley. And it was there I finally shouted, 'Unbind and Return'. It echoed in the hills. And we waited. If it didn't work for some reason, then we'd have to go back – and release the man. He might be a robber but he didn't deserve to die.

We watched the hill above; there the rope would come. A thick cloud was over the top and the wind chilly. After a minute or so and no rope, Smart and I looked to each other. Had the man lied? And then Smart jumped up, pointing with a paw. For there it was, coming out of the cloud like a flying eel, whipping and wriggling down the hillside, until it was back in my grasp. I tied the rope round my waist and we continued.

'He might follow us,' said Smart. 'Now he's free.'

'I don't think so,' I said. 'We've a good distance on him. And he'll be hobbling for a couple of days, those ropes were tight.'

We were in rocky hills so I had the opportunity to try out the rope as we continued. 'Climb and Bind' sent it up a cliff face. 'Over and Bind', across a chasm. The man had not lied.

We walked all morning and then stopped by a stream for a midday meal. There I attempted something new. I dangled the rope in the water and waited until a fish came by. I shouted, 'Surround and Bind' – and the rope twirled round the fish, and I pulled it from the stream. Smart pounced upon it and had half for his lunch.

Having eaten, we continued on our way. Up hills, down into valleys. There was no one about but sheep. It was a pleasant journey, but difficult not to think about the end of it. The Spider of Yoot. And our lack of plan.

It was mid afternoon when I heard the cry. We were climbing upwards and I could see a small house ahead. It was one-storey, white walled with a slate roof. There was a black goat tied up at the side, eating hay. And then the cry came again.

'Oh please help me, somebody help me!'

It was a woman's voice and coming from the back of the cottage. Smart and I ran past the goat, who took no notice of us and continued eating, and went round to the back of the house. There was a vegetable garden, well kept, with cabbages, lettuce, carrots, peas and a high row of runner beans on poles.

The voice was coming from behind them.

'Oh please, help me!'

We ran down the garden and saw an old woman dressed in black, her hair covered in a red headscarf. She was standing by a well that had a low wall round it; she was looking down and wailing. When she saw us coming, she ran to us.

'Oh please, save my daughter!'

I ran to the well and looked down. About halfway, I could see a ledge with something on it, then at the bottom a girl with all but her head in the water, clinging on to the sides.

'My magic book fell in,' wailed the old lady. 'And my daughter went down on the bucket to get it. And the rope snapped.' She shook her fists in agitation. 'It's all my fault; I saw the rope was getting frayed, and should have changed it.'

I uncurled our rope from around my waist. I stepped up on to the wall of the well. I put the end of the rope on to the axle of the well. And said, 'Surround and Bind.'

The rope twisted round the axle. And I took the end, and holding tight, I began to climb down into the well. As I went down the rope grew longer. The well was narrow and I was able to walk down the wall as if down a wide chimney. I looked up, and there was Smart and the old lady gazing down below a circle of sky. Halfway down, I came to the ledge where the book lay. I left it and continued. The girl was more important than a book.

I wondered how long the rope could go on stretching itself. All the way to the moon? But certainly down to the bottom of the well.

'I could not hold on much longer, sir,' said the girl weakly as I neared her.

She was as pale as whey and shivering. Obviously too feeble to climb back up. So I got into the water myself. The cold was a shock; I was not able to touch bottom. And so had to keep one hand on the rope, making it difficult to pass it under her arms to secure her. But in the end I managed it – and she grasped the rope.

'I must climb back up,' I said. 'Then pull you out.'

'Please be quick,' she said, 'before I die of cold.'

And so I made my way back up, pulling myself up on the rope with my feet on the walls. This was harder than coming down. Although I could walk up the wall, I had my weight to carry. But gradually I came up, arm over arm, my feet walking against the sides. Halfway up,

I got the magic book from its ledge, put it under one arm and set off upwards with the extra weight.

At last I came to the top. I handed over the book to the old lady and stepped out of the well, my arms aching. But there could be no rest. The two of us then turned the handle of the well axle and drew the girl up. I hoped I had tied the rope securely, for she was sagging on the rope like a rag doll, no longer holding on. As she slowly came up, I prayed she wouldn't slip out, for it would be a long drop back into the water.

But finally she was out, wet and unconscious. We carried her into the house and onto her bed. It was a one-roomed cottage, and so Smart and I waited outside while the old lady wiped her daughter down and put her to bed.

We were then invited in. The girl was sleeping in the bed. The old lady thanked us profusely and sat us by the fire. She gave me a towel for I needed to dry out, having been in the well. Then food was given to us, and while eating broth and bread, the old lady insisted we stayed the night, which we were only too happy to do.

After a couple of hours, the daughter woke. She was weak, a little shivery, but would recover in a day or so. We ate our next meal round her bed. And while her mother spooned her soup, I ate a thick stew of garden vegetables with plenty of bread and butter, while Smart had the rest of the fish we had caught earlier that day.

I told them of our mission.

The old lady shook her head. 'Many have come this way and not returned.'

'Don't go,' said the daughter.

'I am determined,' I said.

'Why?' said the girl.

'Because a baker's boy doesn't get many chances,' I said.

'You only need one to die,' said the old lady.

'I am determined,' I repeated.

The old lady sighed and said, 'As you will not listen, I will give you something that may assist you.'

She went across the room to a set of shelves full of bottles, jars, jugs and boxes. She took down a small glass bottle with a white powder in it. It was very like a salt cellar as it had small holes in the silvered top.

She handed it over to me. 'Carry it with care,' she said. 'One sprinkle, and whoever receives the dust will become half size.'

'Can they be reverted?' I said.

The old lady smiled. 'I can do it. But make sure you wish it. Some things are better left small.'

I thanked her for the gift.

Smart and I slept the night by the fire. I had sufficient blankets and a pillow for my head. And was well rested by morning. We breakfasted and then left, thanking them for their hospitality.

The old lady said, 'It is for me to thank you. And never can it be enough for bringing my daughter back. Should I ever be able to assist you, please don't hesitate to ask.'

We left them with our good wishes.

Chapter 10

It was as well that we'd had a good breakfast and slept, for most of the day was spent climbing upwards. The old lady had renewed our food stock, so we were well provisioned. She had asked us to stop on the way back, and the look in her eye said 'if'. A feeling I felt myself but it didn't help saying it out loud.

We came into a mist. And the cold clutched at us. I wrapped the blanket round my shoulders and it flapped in the wind like a sail. We could barely see ten yards ahead. There was only one trail up the mountain the old lady had told us, and we must stick to it or risk losing ourselves. Then it would be easy enough in the mist to fall over an edge, or become so lost we would die of exposure.

Ahead was a dark shape, right on our trail. And it was coming towards us. Smart and I stopped. It was taller than a man and coming steadily. Smart's fur was standing up, his tail in the air. I took my dagger from my belt. I held the rope in my other hand.

And then it came out of the mist. It was a black horse, with saddle and blanket but riderless. By its leather and metal work, the horse of a knight. It was followed by a donkey, packs still on its back. But no sign of a human owner.

The animals stopped by us. I could tell they were hungry. I opened the donkey's pack and found some oats, which I poured out onto a flat rock. We left them eating greedily. Likely, they would continue down and come to the old lady's cottage – where I am sure she would have a use for the animals. Or perhaps not, having had too many in the past. If so, she could sell them.

Smart and I did not discuss the fate of the owner.

It began to rain heavily. And soon we were as wet as washing. Ahead though, there was a cave. We scurried into its entrance. And went a little way in to stay out of the driving rain. There, scattered about the rocky floor was armour – helmets, gauntlets, shields, swords, knives – enough to service a small army.

We had arrived at the cave of the Spider.

The cave was high, we could only see far in before it disappeared in gloomy shadow. From my pack I took out the lantern and struck the flints. I had some difficulty lighting it and had to go further in to be out of the wind. It caught.

The light flicked on the walls. On the floor, like trail for us to follow, was a litter of armour, weapons, and bones. All that was left of those that had come to seek glory. Were we to join them?

Cautiously we went deeper into the cave.

As we walked though armour and swords carelessly scattered, I thought there had been no need to bring a single weapon. It was all here. All useless. That helmet, that gauntlet, that sword – had been thrown away or dropped in flight. Or worse: spat out as the flesh was sucked off the bones we stepped over.

We turned a bend and could no longer see the entrance behind us. But instead of growing darker, the cavern was filled with a deep blue light that seemed to come out of the rocks. It had the effect of making Smart almost invisible and the rocks as if in deep, inky water. Up ahead was another bend, which made me nervous. For the Spider was ahead – and could surprise us.

'Stop,' whispered Smart.

I stopped.

'Listen,' said the cat.

At first nothing, then a faint rustling up ahead.

'I think the Spider has heard us,' said Smart. 'And is coming.'

'Then let's wait for it,' I said. Pretending more bravery than I felt.

I put the lantern down. There was no further need for it. I had the rope wrapped around my arm, in my belt was the bottle of powder and my knife. I hoped I would have time to use one of them. The discarded armour and weapons on the floor indicated that the Spider came quickly. I might need something bigger than a knife. I bent down to pick up a sword, but it only lifted a few inches; it was stuck in a sort of goo.

I thought I'd try for another one. There was plenty of choice. But my legs barely lifted above the ground; I was stuck too. I tried lifting one foot, then the other. The sticky stuff stretched under me like dough, then pulled my feet back with a thwack.

'I'm stuck,' I called to Smart. 'How are you?'

I could just make him out slinking along the wall.

'It's alright by the edge,' he hissed.

The rustling was louder. It was plain how the knights failed in their quest. Stuck in the goo, the Spider picked them off. Or could have left them to starve, and ate them when they had no fight left. I, too, would be easy meat unless I could get free.

The rustling was closer, the rock underfoot trembling. The Spider must be huge. I thought of Mother, I thought of the Princess. All they would know is that I had not returned. One of the many who had passed the old lady's cottage.

I stretched at the goo. It was like some alive thing playing with me. It would let me lift my feet a little way, then slap them back to the ground. I pulled and I tugged and I fought, but it had me in its grip and wasn't going to let go.

And then I saw the creature.

It had come out of the bend. And stopped. A huge, furry ball with eight hairy legs, the size of an elephant. It must have seen me, that's why it had stopped. There were two twitching domes high at its front. Eyes I thought. Below them a cavernous gap opened and out of it came a slurpy, sucking sound.

The creature was hungry.

Slowly the creature began to walk. The legs, like metal elbows, held the bulging body above the ground as it slurped and sucked its way to an easy victim.

I looked up to the ceiling of the cavern.

'Climb and Bind!' I yelled.

The rope end flew up and gripped the ceiling. And I pulled at the other, trying to drag myself out of the goo. I scrunched my toes in an attempt to fly out, but the stuff stretched and then slapped me back to the ground.

And the creature came on. The eyes plainly focused on me. The mouth focused, the legs and body eager. I was its next crunch.

I took the knife out of my belt, one hand still on the rope: I scrunched my toes, I pulled at the rope and I hacked at the stretchy goo. It was cutting, but oh so slowly.

The creature was almost on me. I could smell rotten meat; there were flies about its mouth and head. Hear the suck and slurp of it, see the hair on the limbs that would push me in. The chamber of mouth hung above my head, liquid dripping, I drew out the bottle to throw powder at the creature just as a leg grasped me round the chest, pinioning my arms to my side. Another limb came round my head, squashing my nose into the stinky hairs. The mouth was dripping onto me. I was helpless, could not use powder or knife, choking, squeezed in the creature's grip, head drawing into its mouth, spit drooling over me like liquid soap.

Then all at once, the creature was writhing. The limbs unwrapped from me, like rope pulled off a spar, and I dropped back into the goo. The creature was bucking up and down. I couldn't make out what had happened. Why had I suddenly been released? And then I saw Smart on the creature's back. His claws digging into the flesh, the Spider mad to throw him off.

Smart was giving me time. I had to use it.

I stretched and hacked at the ligament of goo. And it cut away with rapid chops. And then all of a sudden it snapped back, pulling my shoes off my feet. But I was free, one arm on the rope. I stuck the knife in my belt and began climbing hand over hand. Desperate to be away, terrified any instant the Spider would haul me back. Under me I could hear the thumping as it struggled to throw off Smart. And if it did, then it would be a short end for the brave cat.

I reached the ceiling, arms aching and out of breath. Below me the great furry ball was rising and falling, while high on its back was Smart, gripping on for sheer life, tail and hair raised in its efforts as the creature bounced and shook.

I could not stay up there much longer. I must work quickly if I were to use the time Smart had given me. I took the bottle from out of my belt. And I sprinkled it. The particles floated down like snowflakes and landed on the creature. And, of course, on Smart.

In a whoosh the creature shrank. And was the size of a horse. But in its anger and writhing it didn't seem to realise. I sprinkled more. The particles floated down. And with a whoosh the creature was the size of a dog. I sprinkled again. And it was the size of a cat.

I climbed down the rope. For the creature was too small for me to sprinkle more dust on its back from that height. Once on the ground I leapt to the side, keeping out of the goo. The creature was still writhing, even though it was as small as a cat, for a real cat was on its back – the size of a mouse. I edged round the walls to get as close as possible. Just as I sprinkled I felt something leap onto my shoulder. It was a tiny Smart.

The Spider was down to rat size. Two more sprinkles and it was mouse, then frog size. One more sprinkle. And then I stopped, for now it was true spider size. So I left it to scuttle away.

A voice on my shoulder squealed, 'Look what you've done!'

I took Smart in my cupped hands.

'It won't be for long,' I said. 'I promise.'

'Better not be.'

I put him in my pocket and rescued my shoes. Each one I pulled out with the rope. When I had them both, I put them on, scrunched my toes, and flew, back the way we had come. Out of the blue light, round the bends and into the light of day. Once back on the mountainside I continued my flight. Hadn't I promised Smart I wouldn't be long?

The mist had gone and we were in bright sunlight. All the brighter after the gloom of the Spider's cavern. All the brighter to be alive and leaving that place of death. All the brighter now the Spider of Yoot was shrunk to insect size.

Never had I enjoyed flying so much as coming down that mountain, the wind in my hair, my clothes flapping. Below me were sheep in the pasture and gurgling streams, all unknowing as to what I had done. I was up with the birds in the blue of the sky, a pity to come down. But I had made a promise.

I landed just in front of the cottage. The old lady was pegging out washing. She was so pleased to see me that she embraced me at once, all of which was almost too much for me. We went into the cottage where her daughter was sitting up in bed, clearly on the mend. I drew Smart out of my pocket.

'You said you can reverse the effect of the powder,' I said.

'I can,' she said, 'though it is rather a trial.'

And she took down pots and herbs from her shelves, followed by a mortar and pestle and various bottles. Then placed them on her table and set to work. Clearly, the old lady was going to be some time, so I offered to bake bread while she was busy. And the girl joined me in her dressing gown and made scones. I put Smart by the fire and he slept, for although a very little cat, a cat he still was.

And when we left in the morning he was full size once more.

Chapter 11

Smart and I went down the mountain and back to the castle. We crossed the drawbridge and there were the two queues. A long queue snaking round the wall, the one for petitioners; I knew it would be useless joining that one. By the day's end we'd be nowhere near the front. In fact I recognised some of the people, still there from the time I'd been in that queue.

No thank you. The one for me was appointments. There were five people in front of the fat man's desk. He had his big book, his quill pen in his fist which he dipped carefully into his pot of ink. And it wasn't long before I was before him.

'Name,' he said without looking up, completing the last transaction in his book.

'Will Baker.'

He put down his quill and ran his fat finger down the page. Then looked up at me with a weary sigh, as if I was nothing but trouble.

'There's no Will Baker here.'

I knew there wouldn't be, because I wasn't expected to return. But here I was. And I meant to see the King.

'There isn't,' I said. 'But I have completed the King's mission.'

'And what is that?' said the man stifling a yawn.

'I have fought the Spider of Yoot.'

'And so?' said the man, stifling a yawn, his jowls dripping down his face like a hunting dog's.

'I've come to claim my reward,' I said.

The man shook his head. 'I've got none of that here.' He jabbed at his book with a ringed finger. 'No name. No nothing.' He looked beyond me. 'Next.'

'I risked my life,' I insisted.

'Many people risk their lives every day,' he said. 'What's that to me?' He raised a hand, and flicked his fingers. 'Guard! Remove him.'

'I will see the King,' I yelled.

And in a flash, I sprinkled the man with powder. In a whoosh, he was the size of a small boy, head barely above his desk, and feet unable to reach the ground. The guard who had been approaching, stepped back as I turned on him with my powder.

'What have you done?' yelled the man in a high voice, his little hands waving over his head.

'I wish to see the King,' I said.

And held my bottle over him. He looked up at me in fear, like a naughty infant at an angry parent.

'No more,' he screamed, holding his hands over his head to shield himself. 'Please.'

'I wish to see the King,' I said.

'Of course, anything,' he squeaked. 'Will Baker to see the King. A priority!'

He tried to reach for his quill but his little arms were not long enough. With my help, he was able to scramble onto the desk, find the quill, dip it into his pot of ink, and holding it in his full fist write my name.

He then looked up.

'Please turn me back to my rightful size, kind sir,' he appealed.

'When I have seen the King,' I said.

'Go, please sir,' he indicated the door. To the servant he peeped, 'Make sure Master Will Baker is first in line.'

I was ushered down the corridor. Past the others waiting, to the front. Just as I got there the court door opened and I was pushed in. It was so quick, I barely had time to breathe.

The hall was the same as my last visit: the King down at the end on his throne, well dressed people along the sides, some of them giggling as I entered with Smart. They, no doubt, hoped for more fun today. The King smiled broadly when he saw me enter and made some joke to those nearby who chortled.

I followed the servant up the hall. He stopped a little way before the throne and bowed.

'Master Will Baker, Your Majesty. Back from his mission.'

The servant backed away still bowing and left me before the throne. I bowed.

The King scratched his chin. 'Ah yes, your mission. Remind me what it was.'

'I was sent to the Spider of Yoot, Your Majesty.'

The King flicked his fingers. 'Of course, I remember. Yes, the Spider of Yoot. A most dangerous fellow.'

The courtiers were giggling, some of the women hiding their laughter behind fans.

'And were you successful, Master Will Baker?' went on the King.

I bowed respectfully.

'Yes, Your Majesty, I was. And I have come to claim my reward.'

'And what is that?'

'The hand of your daughter, Your Majesty.'

The laughter stopped dead. There was a gasp. The King scowled.

'The hand of my daughter. Princess May. You wish to marry her?'

I bowed once more. This was not going well. I preferred being laughed at to the silence of the court. But it was too late to go back. And hadn't I been promised?

'Yes, Your Majesty.'

The King was clasping and unclasping his ringed fingers.

'Tell me, boy, what is your living?'

Boy, was it now. I knew I was being pushed down to size.

'I was a baker's boy...' I began.

The King interrupted. 'A baker's boy. I'm sure that's a good job. We all need bread, don't we?'

The court agreed and there were giggles again.

'Even Kings, Your Majesty,' I said.

There was an intake of breath. I was talking back.

'Even Kings,' agreed the King seeming to ignore my slight. 'But tell me, how many baker's boys do you know that have married princesses?' His eyes widened. 'Is it five, ten, twenty, a hundred? Is it commonplace for baker's boys to marry princesses?'

'I don't know of any, Your Majesty.'

'Neither do I,' said the King.

And nor did the court.

'But my mission was successful, Your Majesty.' I bowed lightly.

'Where is the evidence of your success?' he said. 'Have you the head of the Spider of Yoot, baker's boy?'

'No, Your Majesty.'

'Then why should I believe you?' he shouted at me, waving his sceptre. 'Any pipsqueak who comes here, having ridden twice round the royal park, may claim to have despatched any number of beasts. And then ask for my daughter's hand.' He stopped for an instant looking me hard in the eye. 'Evidence, baker's boy.'

'I have none, Your Majesty.'

'And yet, you went with a cat to Yoot, where many a brave knight has met his death. And you, a baker's boy, killed the creature... If so, why did you not chop its head off?'

'I did not kill it, Your Majesty.'

'Ah,' he looked round the court, nodding wisely at them all. 'Now we get to the truth of it. He did not kill it.'

The courtiers murmured to themselves, 'He did not kill it.'

'I shrank it,' I said. Adding quickly, 'Your Majesty. To the size of an ordinary spider.'

'But did not kill it,' the King insisted.

'I rendered it totally harmless, Your Majesty.'

'But did not kill it.' The King looked around the court. 'I seem to remember the mission was to kill the creature.'

The court assented. Everyone was in agreement – it was to kill.

The King continued, a smile of utter contempt on his lips. 'I did not say shrink. Get the flour out of your ears, baker's boy.'

Smart hissed at my side. I bowed and stroked him to calm him down. It's best that cats don't hiss at kings in a temper.

'Mission – a failure,' said the King. 'If it happened at all, it was a failure.'

The court nodded, telling their neighbours: it was a failure.

I was thinking suppose I had stepped on the spider, where would be the evidence then? I would fail whatever I did.

Baker's boys do not marry princesses.

'Shall we let him have another go?' said the King with a wide beam, stretching out his arms to encompass his courtiers. 'A pity,' he went on, 'when the baker's boy tries so hard, to not let him have another attempt. Don't you think?'

The Lords and Ladies were nodding their assent.

'The same reward, Your Majesty?' I asked.

'The very same, Master Will Baker. My daughter's hand. You shall be the very first baker's boy in the Royal Family.'

The court laughed.

'Tell me my mission, Your Majesty.'

'You must...' he thought for a few seconds, sucking his lower lip, then snapped his fingers. 'Yes, I have it. The perfect mission for you to show your loyalty and courage.'

'Please command me, Your Majesty.' I bowed.

'You must bring me the crown of the Ice King.'

The court gasped.

As for myself, I was not expecting to be asked to catch a fish. And I'd never heard of the Ice King. So I gave a sweeping bow.

'Thank you, Your Majesty. It will be my honour to fulfil your wish.'

'Go to my kitchen,' said the King, 'and get your supplies.' He was smirking now, so I knew there was something coming. 'You may after all wish to throw bread rolls at the Ice King. And, if that doesn't work, charge him down with a loaf.'

Laughter in court. And amidst the merriment I was ushered away.

I was led by a servant out into the courtyard, where I rested against the wall to get my breath back. My hair was prickling at the back of my neck. I felt as if I'd just been whipped.

Smart said, 'Why be laughed at like that?'

'I want to marry the Princess.'

'She won't marry you dead,' he hissed.

'I have something to prove,' I said.

'That bakers' boys are stupid?'

I swung out to kick the cat, but he jumped easily away and hissed at me. We glared at each other.

Our eyeballing was interrupted by Marianne and the Princess approaching. People were bowing as she crossed the courtyard with her maid, plainly coming towards me and Smart. When she was close, I too bowed.

'It is an honour to meet you again, Your Highness.'

She smiled at me. 'I am pleased to see you too.'

'Your father behaves no better,' I said.

She sighed. 'That is the way of my father,' she said. 'He enjoys cruel jokes. The crueller the better. There is no one to stop him.'

'I did defeat the Spider of Yoot,' I said.

'I believe you,' she said. 'But you must bring back some evidence. My father doesn't want to believe you. And will take any opportunity of calling you a liar. He finds it funnier that way.'

'Do you think I am a joke?' I said.

'No,' she said.

For a little while neither of us spoke. I looked into her eyes, and she into mine.

'Will you marry me if I succeed?' I said. 'A baker's boy.'

'The bravest in the land,' she said. 'But it is not me you must persuade but my father.'

'Then I must be off on my mission.'

'You should go home,' she said. 'And stay alive.'

I shook my head. 'I have one chance,' I said. 'Or spend my life baking bread. And if I die – think that at least I tried. And if I should triumph...' I stopped and smiled at her.

And she smiled back like the high sun in midsummer.

'Then you will get your reward,' she said. And stepped forward and kissed me on the cheek.

She retreated and I rubbed the spot, mesmerised.

'You will need warm clothing for the land of ice.' She turned to her maid. 'Marianne, take Will to the Royal tailor.'

Marianne curtseyed, 'Yes, Your Highness.' To me she said, 'Please wait here.'

And still dazzled, I watch them walk away. They crossed the courtyard to the Princess' tower. Marianne opened the door and the two of them went in. And for an instant the light went out of the sky.

'I forgot to say Your Highness,' I whispered.

'I wouldn't worry about that,' said Smart.

'Do you think she's in love with me?' I said.

'What do I know about such things?' said the cat with a shrug. 'Give me a scratch.'

I knelt down and scratched Smart between the ears. He twisted his head, purring.

'Now the ribs.'

While I scratched and Smart rolled over, I gazed at the tower where my beloved had her room. The courtyard was busy with servants pushing barrels and men with important papers under their arms. While in the court the King was humiliating someone else. But there was no one at the window.

I sighed. As I did so, the tower door opened. There was Marianne. She beckoned us over. My mission was about to begin.

Chapter 12

Marianne took us to the Royal tailor where I was fitted out with thick woollens. They were ready-mades, not the best of fits — but I did not wish to wait to get handmade clothing. I could roll up the cuffs and bottoms. A muff served Smart for his body coat with a baby's bonnet for his head, though holes had to be cut for his ears. I was given a backpack to carry them. Marianne left us and Smart and I went to the sullen mapmaker and lastly to the kitchen for supplies.

The kitchen workers sniggered at us, word had obviously got about. Earlier the tailors had been halted by Marianne, for when she saw one of them grinning, she asked if he would like to share his merriment. That stopped him for the moment, but I knew they were laughing as soon as we left.

I was glad to leave the castle. The King said I was a fool, so his court agreed with him and so did every servant and dogsbody, eager to please his master. We walked swiftly, to get the castle and its ridiculing ways behind us.

Once up in the hills, and out of sight of the castle, we stopped to eat and have a good look at the map.

'Those mountains,' I said, pointing them out ahead of us. 'We have to go over them.'

'It's a long way,' said Smart.

'We're going to fly.'

When we had finished eating, we put on our warm clothing. I rolled my cuffs and trouser bottoms, and pulled the woolly hat over my ears. I helped Smart into his muff, tied the bonnet over his head after letting his ears out.

'I hate this,' exclaimed Smart, trying to shake the bonnet off.

'Would you rather freeze?' I said.

'Suppose someone saw me,' he said looking about.

But there was no one. And I tried not to grin at the pink baby's bonnet on Smart's head, tied up under his chin. Less embarrassed at being seen, I was uncomfortably hot. For it was a warm day, with the sun wandering through light cloud. But we hadn't dressed for ground level. Smart jumped onto my shoulder. I scrunched my toes and rose at once.

Higher and higher I went. I did not want us to be spotted from the ground. And up with the clouds I could easily be mistaken for a bird. As we neared the height I was aiming for, my body angle became less steep and Smart gradually came down from my shoulder onto my back. I was glad then I was wearing woollens for his claws went deep into my jacket.

Aloft in the cloud, I lay flat on the cool air. As we emerged into a clear blue space, we saw the tiny world below, sheep like mice on a green carpet, houses like tiny boxes. But gone again as we flew into the mist. We were travelling fast, a distance that would have taken us many days on foot, we would cover in half a day.

The wind made talk impossible. And I was glad of the warm clothing, for the icy air crept down my neck until it was almost numb. But I was powerful in the sky. The world so small below, I was like an eagle surveying its prey. I could dive down and take anything I wanted. This was my kingdom.

Higher, I went over a snow-covered mountain range, crested in cloud. Once out of the freezing haze, there ahead, higher still, was another range. And on its topmost peak was the ice castle. The towers and walls sparkled like silver in the sunlight; I could barely look at the dazzle. It stood sheer on the mountainside, a drop of maybe a thousand feet to the meadow below. We would have had great difficulty climbing up to it from below. And any archer in the castle could easily have shot us down as we clung to the rock face.

If archers were needed. For, as we neared, something jumped off the glowing battlement. From this distance it was like a fluttering handkerchief, pulling rhythmically on the wind. I knew we had been seen.

In a little while I could make it out more clearly. A bird of sorts, long necked like a goose, but green, the colour of bracken. The goose grew, as the distance between us closed. It had a lengthy beak and I caught its cry, like the fierce caw of a crow. There was little point flying away as the bird was travelling faster than we were, and would surely catch us. I thought best to face it, rather than be hunted down.

Smart was standing upright on my back, his claws digging through the layers of wool into my skin. I felt his panic; this was a monster, the size of a boat. And we could be certain it was no greeting party. We were the sparrow and there was our hawk. And, as if to show us the truth of this, the bird began to rise, even as it came in our direction. I knew what the bird wanted to do; be above us, then hurtle down upon us like a spear.

So I rose too. And when the bird saw my tactic it climbed still steeper. And so did I. Step for step, as if on joined ladders, we flew upwards. We would meet at the apex. Time was short, that beak could crush my head like a grape. Those claws tear could out my heart.

Caw! Caw!

Its cry, deafening and fearful. I could not fly from it. I could only face the creature.

I drew the rope from round my waist. Judged its distance, and counted the bird in. Beak wide, claws stretched to seize; it would not deviate and neither would I.

'Surround and Bind!' I yelled.

And the rope flew from my grasp. I was glad I wore gloves or I would have suffered rope-burn. Like a snaking arrow it went for the beast. Around the beak, two twists to clamp it shut, then round the neck like rapidly, curling ivy. Round and round it twirled, binding the body and wings, pulling tighter like one of my mother's parcels of buns. Until those wings were pressed to its body.

And the bird fell.

No longer a flying thing. Without wings, the bird tumbled down like a rock pushed off a sheer mountainside. Parcelled up, its beak and talons were useless. I circled aloft, watching the creature drop. The cat's claws in my back eased as the monster shrank in size.

In next to no time, it was as small as a starling. Nor any longer did it seem to be falling, but held in the sky above the lake in the valley, it simply grew smaller. I did not hear the splash, and barely saw it. Round I flew for a minute or so, watching the levelling surface of the lake.

'Unbind and Return,' I yelled.

It was a while before I saw the rope rising out of the valley. I flew about until the rope came to my hand. I bound it round my waist once more. And headed onwards. Behind us the sun was beginning to set – and the castle no longer glowed in its light, but caught the shadow of the clouds.

I wondered whether there had been spectators on the battlements. If so, they would surely be waiting for us. A mist was forming as I came in. Night fell quickly here. And I was as cold as I had ever been. I could not see anyone on the battlements, but the mist made it difficult; they could be waiting to surprise us.

I landed feet first. Smart jumped off my back. There was no one to be seen in either direction on the rampart. It was when I looked below my feet I could see why. For the floor was transparent, and I could see a hall below. And within were feasting men seated both sides of a long table, piled with meat and jugs of ale. They were boisterous, arms flailing, as if they had been eating and drinking all day. We could not hear them through the ice floor, although musicians were playing, and there must have been much shouting. But they could as well been miming players for all we heard. I thought the guard must be down there too, leaving defence to the great bird.

At the head of the table was the King. He was a bearded man in a blue tunic, shouting at his companions, none of whom were listening, his arms thrashing, splashing ale over his neighbours, who splashed back. On the King's head was a gold crown, set about with diamonds. That surely was what I had come for.

Servants were circling the table, filling the cups as soon as they were emptied. How much, I thought, could the King drink before he collapsed in drunken stupor? I would find out, because I intended waiting.

Smart and I crouched at the edge of the battlements. We could see into the hall as it was well lit with lanterns round the walls and with candlesticks on the table, but could hardly be seen ourselves as the sun had set. Perhaps in the twilight, if the revellers cared to look up, they might note two shadows by the wall – but why should drunken men heed those?

But it was cold on the ice floor. We could not move, for that surely would have us seen. Below us the silent feast seemed to go on forever. The stars came out one by one, until the sky was so filled I could not believe there could be so many. Any other time I would have loved to stargaze, but not so frozen. All those lights together had not the warmth of a single candle flame.

Smart shivered by my side, that drunken night. The feast became wilder. Men stumbled about and collapsed into their plates. It seemed that was the goal of everyone, for those with any remaining life drank until they too hit the tabletop. The King lasted longer than most, I suspect he had had more practice, but eventually joined his subjects amidst the remains of food and ale.

Smart and I, at last, rose. I flapped my arms to and fro and jumped up and down. But little warmth came. We must make our way down. The two of us circled the battlements. A half moon had risen to light our way, showing us some icy steps, lightly frosted. As we descended, our prints showed up behind us, boy and cat. The stairs followed the inside wall of the hall where we could see the snoring, prone figures.

At the hall level we found the door easily enough. And went in. The room was foul with beer, sweat, and leavings. These men didn't wash much. Nor was it much warmer in the hall. If the men of the ice castle weren't so clean, they were hardy.

I cautiously walked to the head of the table followed by Smart, not wishing to wake the slumped bodies. Not that they would have made much sense of us if they did. The King's head lay sideways on the table, half in his plate where he'd left almost a whole chop in its gravy. I began easing the crown off his head. The King groaned and rolled in his plate. I stopped, waited and then continued. And then I had it in my hands: a burnished gold crown with a hint of red at the ornate points, each one set with a large diamond that shone in the candlelight.

I turned to leave, and had taken a step or two towards the door when a voice behind me yelled:

'Catch that thief!'

I turned. At the rear door were three guards, the centre one with a spear, the two at his side with bows that they were already filling with arrows. The one with the spear stayed at the door, while the archers advanced.

I began unwinding my rope when I heard a shout behind me.

'Put down that crown!'

There were more coming through that door. I could not fight them all. Nor could I fly off as they held the doors. I would be an easy target up on the ceiling. And so put the crown on the table and raised my hands.

I was at once surrounded and prodded on the by spear men. I was taken out into the corridor while they cursed and pushed me towards a tall, portly man, not in soldier's gear but plainly in charge. They stopped before him. He reminded me of one of the courtiers at my King's court, in his long wine coloured robe and the gold chain round his neck. He slapped me round the face with his ringed hand.

'Thief! Scum!'

He spat in my face, stinking of ale.

My face stung, I could feel a trickle of blood in the spit. But I said nothing. I could not deny being a thief, they had seen me with the crown in my hands. And what was I, a stranger, doing here at all?

'Take him to the dungeon, guards.' As they led me away, he added, 'We'll have his head in the morning.'

I was pushed down icy stairs, guards in front and behind. As we came lower it became darker, even though the walls were of clear ice; curtains and furniture held off the light of the moon and stars. We stopped at a corridor, gloomy in a faint greenish light. A guard lifted a stout plank of ice, and a door was pushed open. I was thrust inside and the door creaked shut behind me.

I was alone in an ice prison. I had not noted Smart going, but he was not with me. What had happened to him? Had he been speared or was he able to get away in the fuss? To where, to do what?

I explored the space.

Four ice walls: the door in one to the corridor, the two side walls through which I could see shadowy forms. Other prisoners I thought. The fourth wall puzzled me, I couldn't make out what there was. It was hazy; there seemed to be drifting smoke. And then for an instant, in a gap that quickly filled, I saw the moon. And understood. It was an outside wall in a jacket of cloud.

There was no furniture, no blankets. On one wall was a raised ice platform that might serve for a bed or a seat. I tried sitting on it, but the cold seeped into my backside, down my legs and up my body. And tired as I was, I rose and walked about my cell. I noted the other shadows, in other cells, walking too.

There was no escape. I must wait till morning, the day of my beheading, and take my chance when they led me elsewhere. In the meantime, I must get through the night. I had my hood up, tied tight under my chin. I thrust my hands up the opposite sleeves and I walked. Round and round the walls until I was weary of walking. Sat until I was frozen with sitting. Stood until I had to walk more to get my blood moving. Cold filled my mind. And the opposite. I had a vision of opening the oven at home and the heat rushing out, full of the yeasty smell of newly baked bread. I dreamt of a hot slice, butter melting into it, as I shivered and clutched my arms to my chest. Later, the cloud cleared from the outside wall, and I could see the moon and stars, my cold companions. My teeth chattered, my fingers and toes were in pain. I was so hungry, frozen and weary.

The night seemed endless. As if dawn were playing tricks, deliberately holding back. A couple of times I thought I saw first signs. But I hadn't, as in a little while it was as black and as bleak as before.

And then it came. First light. But was no warmer. And knew it would not be; for I was in a room of ice where no heat could enter. It meant simply that time passed, even here. I wondered about those shadows in my neighbouring cells. How long had they been there? They must be tougher than me, born to cold, for in a few days I would surely die of it.

At last they came for me.

Four men with spears marched in, bleary eyed and gruff, with crumbs in their beards. And marched me out, two at the rear and two at the front. They directed me up the ice stairs, our footsteps ringing through the castle like morning bells. We came to the level of the hall; miraculously empty, apart from a few servants wiping the table and sweeping the floor. The sleepers had somehow staggered to their beds.

And up to the battlements. The sun was rising in the sky but had little heat still. Our party continued round the battlements, steam puffing from our mouths. We approached a small group that was obviously waiting for us. One was the King, wearing the same robes he wore last night and his crown upon his head. He could barely keep his eyes open, his tongue lolling round his teeth, perhaps to get out the bits of meat or the taste of stale ale.

By the King was a huge man, in black leggings, bald and bare-chested in spite of the cold. He had by his side a massive sword, the long blade sparkling in the sunlight. I had no need to ask its purpose.

The King strode up and pulled back my hood. His eyes were bloodshot and he stank of the banquet.

'Who are you, boy?' he exclaimed.

'Will Baker,' I said.

The King lifted my chin and felt my neck as if he was examining a dead chicken. Behind him, the big man had raised the sword in both hands. He swung it to and fro, his knees bent. I doubted he needed the practice. One swipe was all it would take.

'Goodbye, Will Baker,' said the King. And he stepped back into the circle of men.

I was the centre. The big man circled me, swinging the sword. Over the top, down my body. He was enjoying the show of it. The bulging muscles of his arms and chest had been oiled. He pulled back the sword over his shoulder, eyes on my neck…

A black frenzy dropped out of the sky and on to the head of the King. The crown toppled off his head, and I caught it in my hands, followed immediately by Smart who scrambled onto my shoulder.

The executioner dared not swing his sword as the King was on the ground near me. Guards were stepping forward to grab me… I clicked my heels and rose into the air. Smart settled round my shoulder as I climbed. I must make all speed as arrows would come shortly. I did not look back at the activity below though I could hear the yelling. After a few seconds I dived, and arrows passed over my head. Then up I came; by the time they could shoot again I would be away. But just in case, I twisted about. The salvo flew by, closer than I would have liked – but I was drawing out of range. And the next arrows did not reach me.

There were angry cries behind, lessening as I put distance between us.

I settled flat on the wind, and made my own speed. They could not follow. Their bird was dead. Smart made himself more comfortable on my back. In my hands I carried the crown of the Ice King. This time there would be evidence. No one could say I hadn't completed my mission.

I settled into the flight.

It was half a day back. Over the mountains, down into the valleys, over hills and on to the castle. I would be glad to be away from the cold, and to eat again. I wondered where Smart had been all night, and where he'd been to make that dive onto the King, but we could not speak.

On I flew throughout the morning, over the snow-capped mountains and then down into the valley where thankfully it was warmer. We stopped for a while on a hillside in full sun. It was heaven to be warm again. I drank from a stream and then lay back and enjoyed the heat. I shut my eyes and let them warm in the red glow.

'The crown!' hissed Smart.

I shook myself and opened my eyes. And looked to the rock where I had left the crown. I couldn't understand. It was dripping, but I hadn't put it in the stream. I rose and picked the crown up. And at once it was clear.

The crown of the Ice King was melting.

Chapter 12

Back at the castle I went straight to the queue for appointments. It was as short as usual. And in less than ten minutes I was at its head. And there was the man at his desk, as small as I had left him, seated cross-legged upon his desk with the quill in his fist.

'Will Baker,' I said. 'To see the King.'

He put his hands together in a plea. 'Please, Master Baker, return me to my rightful size.'

He was pitiful, in the same proportion as before, as fat and as jowly, but half the size. No longer able to work from his chair.

I said, 'When I have seen the King.'

He pulled at my coat. 'You promise me, sir? You will not leave me this way?'

I jerked away.

'I promise.'

He scrawled whatever he had to in his book, and then yelled in his squeaky voice, 'Master Will Baker – next in line to see the King. Priority! Take him to the front.'

And I was rushed away.

Into the short hallway, past the others who had been ahead of me. Straight to the front of the queue. And at the second of my arrival, the door of the court opened and I was ushered inside.

I bowed as I entered. I knew well enough what to do. This was my third visit. Bow once more when I got to the throne, and bow whenever I finished speaking.

Merriment at once greeted me. I was a popular turn. I expect much of their day must be dull. And the baker's boy really lightened their time.

'Back so soon?' said the King.

I bowed.

'I have completed my mission, Your Majesty,' I said.

'Remind me what it was,' said the King.

'It was to bring back the crown of the Ice King.'

The King smiled, but I knew that smile, there was little friendliness in it.

'I don't actually see the crown,' said the King. 'Perhaps your little animal has swallowed it.'

The King chortled as he said this, finding it very funny, and so did the court.

Smart hissed. I bowed and stroked his back, feeling the tenseness. He hated it here as much as I did.

'If you have brought the crown,' said the King, 'please be so kind as to show it to us.'

I looked at Smart who looked back at me. I had been expecting this, nevertheless I wasn't comfortable. But I had to do it.

I took my glove out of my pocket.

'The crown, Your Majesty.'

I wrung out the glove, until there was a puddle on the court floor.

'That is not a crown,' said the King. 'That is a pool.'

The King's joke was repeated among the courtiers. 'Not a crown...but a pool.'

I bowed.

'That puddle, Your Majesty, is the crown of the Ice King.' I looked about me. Every eye was on me – had I gone mad? I added, 'The Ice King had a crown of ice.'

I said no more but it would not have been heard above the laughter. It went on for perhaps half a minute and then the King held up his bejewelled hands for silence. It came immediately.

'Another failure, baker's boy.' He shook his head as if sadly. 'Failure upon failure.'

'It is the crown,' I said firmly.

'It is a pool,' said the King.

'It is the crown.'

The King flicked his fingers. 'Seize him guards!'

Two guards ran from the door.

I pulled out the rope from round my waist.

'Surround and bind!'

The rope whipped out to the guards, twirled round and round them, until they were so bundled up that they collapsed on the floor.

Two more guards ran in. And I clicked my heels and was up in the air. The guards ran below me, while I flew on, above the King's throne.

'I claim my reward,' I shouted to the King.

'Seize him, guards!'

And so I sprinkled the powder. The dust dropped on the King's head and shoulders, and in an instant he had shrunk to the size of a child. His feet were off the ground, and his body halfway down the back of the throne.

'I claim my reward!' I shouted once more.

'Seize him, guards!' came the King's tiny voice.

But I waved my cellar, and the guards kept their distance. So I sprinkled it once more on the King. He put his hands over his head, but it dusted him enough. And in instant he had shrunk until he was the size of a chicken.

'Enough!' he yelled in panic.

'I claim my reward!'

The Princess stepped out from the courtiers.

'Please, Will, let that be enough.'

I landed on the ground in front of her.

'Will you marry me?' I said.

She nodded. 'Yes, Will. But you must change my father back.'

'After we are married,' I said.

The Princess looked at her tiny father, and smiled.

'Very well,' she said. 'He will be less trouble with the arrangements.'

'Please change me back,' said the King in the tiniest of voices. 'I agree to everything.'

'When we are married, Father,' said the Princess firmly. 'Please don't be unpleasant before we have even begun the arrangements.'

And that was how it happened. How I came to marry the Princess. It was a grand wedding, everybody who was anybody came; even the tiny king, who hated every minute.

'Do be quiet, Father,' his daughter kept saying.

And for a man used to being instantly obeyed, this was humiliating. But then he'd been cruel enough to others, so a little humiliation was fitting. After the wedding came the banquet, and only after that did I see about getting the King back to his rightful size. You see, I had invited the witch and her daughter, the one I'd rescued from the well. And I asked them, if they would be so kind as to revert the King to his proper size. And while they were at it – might they do the man in charge of appointments?

They were happy to do so. But it was quite a rigmarole. It took some time, what with all the strange ingredients they needed. I told them there was no hurry. Little kings made less noise. My mother came to the wedding of course. She was invited to be the Royal baker — but she said she preferred our village. And considering some of the courtiers, I could understand that.

But every Royal castle needs a royal cat. And I don't need to tell you who got that job.